Savage Spirit

In the DAWN OF LOVE series

Reckless Heart
Wild Prairie Sky
Savage Spirit
Fearless Love
Defiant Dreams
Promise Forever

MEG CAMERON

Savage Spirit

DRAGON
GRAFTON BOOKS
A Division of the Collins Publishing Group

LONDON GLASGOW
TORONTO SYDNEY AUCKLAND

Dragon
Grafton Books
A Division of the Collins Publishing Group
8 Grafton Street, London W1X 3LA

Published in Great Britain by Dragon Books 1986

First published in USA by Archway Paperback,
an imprint of Pocket Books, Simon & Schuster, Inc.,
New York 1985

British Library Cataloguing in Publication Data

Cameron, Meg
Savage spirit.——(Dawn of love; 3)
I. Title II. Series
813′.54[F] PS3553.A43/

ISBN 0-583-30901-1

Printed and bound in Great Britain by
Collins, Glasgow

Set in Times

Chapter 1

'Cat! They're starting!'

Catherine Brant raced to the little loft window and bent double to look out. The yard was crowded with people – the whole settlement had turned out for her brother George's wedding.

'The fiddlers are here,' Ike Brent called up to her in an excited voice.

'And I snuck a rum punch for you,' James added, showing her a mug held close against his vest.

'Shh,' Ike hissed, digging his elbow into his brother's ribs. 'You want everyone to hear you?'

Cat laughed down at her two favourite brothers. 'Well, save at least a little for me,' she called. She backed away from the window, remembering that her bodice still had to be laced. 'There, you see,' Cat said with grim satisfaction as she turned to her mother. 'It's starting, and you've been fussing over me so long I'm not even dressed yet. Oh, I'm going to miss *everything*.'

Mrs Brant was an equal match for her daughter. As if they had all the time in the world, she began to draw the long pink ribbon through the double row of eyelets that ran up Cat's back. 'You're not going to miss anything at all,' she said calmly. 'They can't start without the bride, and Mary's still downstairs.'

'Poor Mary!' Cat said with sudden passion. All morning long Aunt Chess and Aunt Fox had been arguing over every article of clothing the bride put on. 'Poor Mary – she's just like butter in a churn to them. They'll turn her inside out before they're finished. If she had a mind of her own, she'd get out of this family now, while there's still time.'

Mrs Brant tied the bodice laces – a double knot, so Cat wouldn't loosen them. 'Girls with minds of their own usually don't get husbands,' Cat's mother said, her meaning unmistakable.

Cat gave an unconcerned shrug. 'Girls with minds of their own usually don't *want* husbands,' she replied.

'Stay still a minute,' Mrs Brant said.

Cat squirmed as her mother fluffed the puffed sleeves that reached to her elbows, where they ended in rows of pointed frills. 'Can I go now?' she asked impatiently. Such a fuss over one little dress!

'No,' Mrs Brant told her, and added, 'I suppose you'd be just as happy to go to your brother's wedding in buckskins.'

'I would!' Cat cried, lifting her chin as her mother began to brush her tumbling dark blonde hair. 'And George wouldn't mind it, either.'

'Well, *I'd* mind,' Mrs Brant said. 'Just once, I'd like to remember I'd raised a girl along with the boys.' She pushed Cat gently away and held her at arm's length. 'There. The Lord himself wouldn't know you.'

Cat's eyebrows went up. 'Oh? Do I look that bad?'

Her mother's face was fresh as spring when she smiled. 'You look beautiful,' she said. 'Go and see.'

But Cat didn't stop to look into the pewter disc mirror that hung downstairs. She ran out into the yard, her pink skirt bouncing out from her waist to show a drift of white petticoats.

'Where's my punch?' she asked, catching James by the elbow.

'Ike drank it,' James said.

Ike was tall and thin and quick. He caught James by the collar before he could dash away. 'You're a terrible liar,' he said. 'You drank it yourself.'

Cat ignored their squabbling. Her eyes sorted through the crowd. 'Why's everybody looking at me?' she asked suddenly. 'Is my skirt turned up or something?'

Ike shrugged. 'I guess they don't recognize you without your squirrel-hunting clothes on, Cat.'

'Maybe they never even knew we *had* a sister,' James suggested, his brown eyes dancing. 'The seven Brant brothers, that's who we are!'

Cat tossed her head. It was strange to feel her hair, hanging loose instead of in braids, sweep against her back. 'The seven *daring* Brant brothers,' she corrected. Above the crowd she heard a thin, tantalizing wisp of fiddle music. 'I wish they'd start,' she said. 'Where's Pa?'

'The Major's over there,' Ike said. Cat followed her brother's glance to a cluster of men. Her father's back soared above them. He was wearing the jacket he'd worn fighting against the British, a brave blue thing with brass buttons and a gold fringe at the shoulders.

'It's a wonder the British didn't get him, isn't it?' James asked. 'What a target he must have made!'

Cat giggled. 'Get Pa?' she asked. 'They wouldn't have dared.'

A sudden commotion filled the air, and Cat saw

three more of her brothers – Joshua, Deland, and William – spill around the corner of the house and land against one of the long tables filled with food. 'The Major's going to give it to them,' Ike said, with authority. Now that George was getting married and moving to a cabin a quarter-mile away, Ike was the oldest, the next in command.

Cat saw her father's heavy eyebrows fly up like startled crows. Ike was right – the Major really *would* give it to them if they started rough-housing now.

'I'm going to go see if Mary's ready,' Cat said lightly. She skimmed towards the house. Inside, behind the curtain they'd hung up, she found her two aunts and her future sister-in-law.

'What do you think of her hair?' Aunt Chess asked, taking Cat by the elbow.

'It looks fine,' Cat said quickly.

Aunt Chess shot Aunt Fox a triumphant look. 'Just as I've been telling you,' she said.

Mary turned large, helpless brown eyes on Cat, who snatched the brush away from Aunt Chess and laid it on the table. 'Everyone's waiting,' she said. 'Come on.'

Aunt Chess led Mary out into the sunlit yard. Aunt Fox hung back. 'You're twice the beauty she is,' Pa's oldest sister whispered to Cat. 'Brant blood – it shows every time.'

Cat didn't pay any attention to her. Both her aunts had been notorious flirts in their day – neither of them the tomboy that Cat herself was.

The ceremony, everyone said later, was exactly what a wedding ceremony should be: sweet as a summer day, short as a winter one. Mary wore a dress of yellow brocade, and George stood up in a peach-coloured coat and blue trousers. When the new couple turned away from the minister everyone cheered. Fiddle music filled the air, and a ring formed for dancing.

Cat smiled, and a single dimple showed on her left cheek. 'Oh, dance with me, won't you, Ike?' she asked excitedly. George and Mary were already in the centre of the ring, and the other couples were starting to join them.

'Not me, Cat,' Ike said. 'Get James.'

Cat turned to her other favourite. James, husky and fun-loving and just a year younger than she was – surely *he* wouldn't turn her down. But he did, and Cat's smile vanished. 'Well, if you won't dance with me, I don't want to be with you at all, either one of you!' she cried and flounced off.

She walked straight to the food table and ate three jam tarts. Her father found her with a pouting face and sticky fingers. 'What's wrong with you, m'lady?' he asked, his dark eyes crinkling when he smiled.

Cat licked her fingers. 'Ike and James won't dance with me.'

Major Brant smiled. 'Won't they, now? Well then, will you dance with your father?'

Cat's face lit up. She made the kind of deep curtsy she imagined the ladies in Washington and Baltimore made. 'Delighted,' she said.

Cat felt light as a leaf on her father's arm. He was tall and powerful, and the wings of grey at his temples only made him look more distinguished.

Like everyone else in the little settlement of

Brant's Orchard, Cat believed that her father could do anything. He had fought the British without getting a scratch, and then, after the war, he had led over a dozen families to this spot on the banks of the Cumberland River. He had even won over the Shawnee, whose villages spread to the west and the north. They had been hostile and suspicious at first, but he told them he was bringing a trading post along with the cabins and the barn sheds. The Indians kept their distance that first season, Cat remembered, but at winter's end they came to trade their furs for knives, pots, guns, and calico. They had kept up a steady commerce since then, and Cat, like her brothers, grew up learning a fair amount of the Shawnee language.

The fiddle music stopped too soon. Cat could have danced on and on, swept along in the clear stream of the music. She tugged at her father's hand. 'Dance with me again, Pa,' she urged.

Major Brant wiped his brow. 'Later Cat,' he told her.

Cat frowned. 'But I love to dance, and if you don't dance with me, no one will!' she protested.

'I'll dance with you, Cat,' someone said.

Cat turned. It was Ike's friend, Tom Alexander. She looked at him doubtfully. 'Can you dance?' she asked.

The fiddle music was lacing through the trees again. 'Try me,' he said, grinning and bobbing his head so that the sun bounced off his copper-coloured hair.

Cat laughed and gave him her hands. 'I wish you'd teach my brothers something about dancing,' she said.

‘Why?’ Tom questioned.

‘So they’d dance with me, of course.’

‘Oh, but I wouldn’t do that – then I wouldn’t get to dance with you myself.’

Cat looked at him uncertainly, then she laughed. She’d always liked Tom. Along with Ike and James, he’d taught her how to shoot squirrels and set fishing lines. He was like another brother to her, even if he was looking at her today in a confusing kind of way. At weddings, Cat thought, people said and did things they didn’t mean. It was the big barrel of rum punch back in the shade that caused it all.

She danced three times with Tom Alexander and then two times with Elias Singer. Matt Hammond asked to dance with her, and Jericho Wales said he’d give a gold piece to be her partner. Tom came back and said he’d give Jericho two gold pieces to leave her alone.

Cat laughed as she went from partner to partner. She had never had so much fun. Imagine – dancing every dance instead of being left outside of things with the children and old people! Her face glowed with excitement, and her blue eyes lit up every corner of the yard. No one was looking at the bride anymore – they were looking at Cat.

‘You’re an angel,’ Tom Alexander said the fifth time he danced with her.

Cat inhaled sharply, testing the air for the give-away scent of rum. There wasn’t any, and she didn’t know what to say. ‘I’m just me,’ she said. ‘Cat.’

Tom smiled at her and looked into her eyes so steadily that Cat began to blush. That only made things worse, because then Tom said, ‘You look just like a rose.’

She wished he would decide what she was – an angel or a rose. She'd rather just be herself.

The sun slipped down behind the trees, but the fiddlers kept the music going. Cat danced until her hair hung hot against her neck. She snatched up the gauzy blue scarf her mother had tucked into the scooped-out neckline of her dress and used it to tie her hair back. She danced two more dances this way, then caught her mother's beckoning eye. 'I'll be right back,' she told Tom.

Her mother caught her elbow and pulled her into the cabin. 'What's got into you?' she asked, tugging the scarf from her daughter's hair. She smoothed the blue gauze over Cat's shoulders and tucked the ends into the low neckline of the dress. 'You can't show the whole world your neck. You'll be sixteen soon – you're not a child anymore.'

Cat looked down at the white curves of her breasts, hidden under the clouds of blue gauze. It was no good telling her mother she hadn't stopped to think. 'Yes, Ma,' she said. 'Can I go back out now?'

'You keep that kerchief where it belongs, Cat.'

'Yes, Ma.'

She'd almost escaped when Aunt Fox and Aunt Chess caught her. 'You're doing mighty fine for yourself today,' Aunt Chess said knowingly.

Cat looked at her. 'I like to dance,' she said.

The two aunts winked at each other. 'She loves to *lead* a dance, that's what I say,' Aunt Fox said proudly. 'A Brant through and through. And do you know, she looks just like I did when I was fifteen.'

Aunt Chess's lips puckered. 'She looks like *me* if

she looks like anyone. Your hair never was blonde thataway, and you know it. More of a creek-bottom brown, it was.'

Aunt Fox sniffed and turned her back on her sister. 'Don't pay her any mind,' she told Cat. 'You've inherited the Brant way with men, sure enough. You won't ever have to worry about getting a husband – not with Tom Alexander hooked the way he is.' Aunt Fox winked slyly. 'All you have to do is reel him in.'

Hot colour rose in Cat's cheeks. 'But Tom's my friend!' she protested. 'We were just dancing together – it doesn't mean anything.'

The two aunts exchanged knowing looks. 'Everything means something, hon,' Aunt Chess said.

Cat stamped her foot. 'Well, *that* doesn't. Besides, I'm not going to get married at all.' She swirled out of the cabin, her aunts' laughter echoing behind her.

Clouds of dust rose in the yard, and Cat saw the rumps of horses retreating through the woods. 'Where's everyone going?' she asked Tom.

'To George and Mary's cabin – we're going to shivaree them.'

Cat's eyes sparkled. A shivaree – banging pots and pans outside the couple's new house and whooping like a hundred Shawnee. Now she could pay George back for all the times he'd tickled and teased her. 'Are you going?' she asked.

''Course,' Tom said. 'You can come along with the women – I'll see you there.'

But the women were walking through the woods on foot. By the time they got to the new cabin, the fun would be over. That wouldn't do at all. George was her own brother. She wanted to be right there banging on his walls and screaming like an Indian at him. Cat smiled up at Tom. 'Take me with you, Tom,' she said. 'Please?'

Tom smiled back at her. 'Sure thing, Cat.' He mounted his horse and pulled her up in front of him. His arms went around her to hold the reins.

They started off through the woods at a trot, following one of the little paths that led from the Brant cabin. The leaves on the trees were still the light green colour of spring, and the woods smelled damp and fresh.

Cat sat up straight. 'Tom, this is the wrong way,' she said. 'George and Mary's cabin is west of ours, not east.'

Tom chuckled. Cat felt his cheek brush against her. 'I know, Cat,' he said.

Chapter 2

Tom Alexander's horse darted and swerved between the trees. Cat might have fallen had Tom's arms not tightened around her. He caught her snugly to him and held her captive in his arms.

Cat had known Tom all her life, but suddenly she felt as if she didn't know him at all. His voice was strange in her ears, and his breath was warm and eager against her neck. And strangest of all were the tingling, shivery sensations that raced through her whenever Tom touched her.

Cat cleared her throat, trying to clear away her confusion. 'George and Mary's cabin is yonder ways,' she told Tom again, pointing in the direction they had just come.

Tom reined the horse to a halt and slid down from the saddle. He caught Cat by the waist and pulled her down after him. 'Oh, Cat!' he burst out, his face red with feverish excitement. 'You're the prettiest girl I ever saw. I been watchin' you all afternoon, hardly believin' you was the same Cat I'd growed up with. The minute I saw you in that dress, I knew – I knew – '

Before Cat realized what was happening, Tom surged towards her, his brown eyes shining and eager. He swept her into his arms, sending shivery ants dancing up her arms again. For a minute Cat forgot who he was. She forgot that he was her brothers' best friend and like a brother to her as well. She forgot everything except the warm, delighted feeling that was taking hold of her body.

Tom's arms closed around her, and Cat made no move to resist him. She had read a novel once, a thick stack of pages that kept you reading to see what would happen next. What was happening now was like that novel. Her curiosity pulled her along. More than anything else, she wondered what would happen next.

Cat was still wondering when Tom pushed close against her. His mouth clamped down on top of hers, and the shivery feeling inside her rose up like an ocean wave. She grabbed at him to keep from toppling over. She had never been kissed before. Even with a boy like Tom, who was just a friend, it was exciting. What would it be like, she wondered, to kiss someone you loved?

Cat tried kissing Tom back and discovered that kissing was almost as much fun as being kissed. When she finally pulled away from him, she saw a look of blissful delight on Tom's face. 'It's certain, then,' he said. 'You feel the same way I do 'bout things.'

She didn't catch the meaning of his words – not until he pulled her to him again and murmured into her hair, 'I love you, Cat. I sure enough mean to marry you.'

Cat jerked back in horror. She realized that she'd made a terrible, terrible mistake. No one had even held her hand before today, much less said he loved her. Yet here was Tom Alexander, expecting to marry her. And all because she'd let him kiss her! Cat forced herself to be calm, to treat Tom in the same friendly, joking way she always had. 'Oh, you wouldn't want to marry me, Tom,' she said lightly. 'I can't cook a lick, and you'd starve for certain.'

Tom reached for her. 'You'd learn to cook, Cat. Most girls do, once they're – '

She cut him off before he could say the word *married.* 'I don't know what's gotten into you to talk this away, Tom,' she said. 'I believe you must have been drinking that rum punch with my brothers. It makes people talk all sorts of nonsense.'

Tom looked hurt. 'I haven't touched a drop, Cat. And I'm not talking nonsense at all. I love you. I want to marry you.'

Cat had had enough of her novel-reading curiosity. She had no desire at all to find out what would happen next. Quick as lightning, she slipped out of Tom's reach and hopped up on to his horse. 'I'm going to George and Mary's shivaree,' she called to him, flicking the horse into a trot. 'I expect you'll get there on foot all right.'

Tom ran along behind her, calling out for her to stop. But Cat rode almost a half-mile before she reined the horse to a halt. Even then, she only let Tom climb up behind her on the understanding that he would not, under any circumstances, utter the terrible word *marriage* to her again.

Cat didn't know what had got into Tom Alexander. Her aunts thought they knew, though. They came visiting a few days after George's marriage, curious as racoons about what had happened between Cat and Tom.

'Nothing at all happened,' Cat said, trying to keep the blush she felt from showing in her cheeks. 'I don't know what you're talking about.' But she didn't dare meet her aunts' inquiring eyes, and she felt, rather than saw, the look they exchanged behind her back.

How do they know? Cat wondered as she lifted the dasher in the butter churn and plunged it down into the half-made butter. The idea that her wily old aunts might have guessed that she'd kissed Tom Alexander made her cheeks red as autumn apples. Cat was quite certain that, flirts though her aunts had been, neither of them had ever had a kiss quite so thrilling as the one she'd had with Tom. They would never understand how it had carried her along, filling her with excitement that evaporated as quickly as morning dew. No, to them, a kiss could only mean one thing: marriage. It galled Cat to know that Aunt Chess and Aunt Fox were in total agreement with Tom on the subject of kissing.

'Has Tom been by to walk out with you?' Aunt Fox inquired, her old eyes bright and beady. *Walking out* meant courting. A boy who liked you came to your house and asked your father if he could take you out walking. Cat had never walked out with anyone before. Sometimes she pictured the kind of boy she would like to walk out with, but that boy was nowhere to be found in Brant's Orchard. 'I bet he has been by,' Aunt Fox added, with a bold wink at Aunt Chess.

''Lessen he's too shy,' Aunt Chess put in, touching her hand to her dust cap and arranging the ruffle.

Cat glared at her aunts. 'Tom Alexander *hasn't* been by,' she said, her arms rhythmically lifting the dasher and plunging it down. 'Nor will he. Not to walk out, anyways. Tom and I are friends, and there's an end to it,' She pulled the dasher up and began scraping the sweet, flower-yellow butter off the paddles.

Aunt Fox's laugh crackled through the air. 'Then I reckon my eyes is gettin' worse than I thought, for I could swear that's him ridin' up the lane now.'

Cat flew to the window, but Aunt Chess, plump yet solid as a log pile, pushed her out of the way. 'You run off and fix yourself, Cat,' she commanded. 'You got to look your best when a young man comes to walk out with you.'

That was how Tom Alexander came to walk out with her for the first time. When he came back four more times in the next two weeks, all of Brant's Orchard took notice. And the more Cat tried to discourage him, the more often he came to visit.

Tom Alexander was a study in stubborn determination. When Cat told him that she didn't love him, he only replied that *he* loved *her*. When she told him that she didn't know pinfeathers about keeping house, he told her that she'd learn. When she went to the drastic extreme of telling him that she didn't expect to get married to anyone *ever*, he began, all over again, to tell her how he had fallen in love with her.

It had all happened the minute he saw her in the pink dress. 'You looked just like a flower in the springtime in that dress, Cat,' Tom would say, awkwardly twisting her fingers in his own. 'I said to myself right then that I had to marry you.'

Cat almost felt sorry for him. How could a boy as ordinarily smart as Tom lose his senses over a dress? She couldn't explain that just listening to him talk such silliness made her want to jerk her hand away, just as she couldn't explain that the kiss she'd given him hadn't been a gift to him but to herself.

So she sat with him or walked out with him whenever he came, not wanting to hurt his feelings by refusing to see him but not knowing what else to do. All the time Tom talked, her sharp little mind clicked and whirred. If she didn't think of a way to discourage him soon, she's find herself swept right up to the altar.

It didn't help that Cat's brothers found the matter prime material for merriment. Joshua, younger than her by five years, would roll his eyes up till only the whites showed and pretend to swoon at her feet. The whole family laughed at this impression of poor, love-struck Tom. Deland and William, the two youngest, would follow Cat and Tom into the woods whenever they walked out. More than once, Cat had spied out the curious blue eyes of her little brothers hidden among the leaves.

Only Ike and James tempered their amusement with understanding. 'Don't worry, Cat,' they promised her between gusts of laughter. 'We'll protect you from him. If he tries to carry you off, we'll ride after and bring you back.'

'Promise?' Cat asked, though she prayed things wouldn't go that far.

Tom Alexander was *her* problem, one Cat felt honour-bound to solve by herself. If words weren't enough to discourage him, she reasoned, perhaps looks and actions were.

The next time she saw Tom's horse jogging up the lane, Cat ran to put on her oldest buckskin shirt and britches. They were patched and stained and smeared with the smell of gutted fish and squirrel.

If my looks don't keep him away, Cat thought with a grin, *my smell ought to.* As she thought this, she wound her long, honey-coloured hair into a coil and jammed a fur cap down on top of it. *I hate to do this to you, Tom,* she thought, *but it's for your own good as well as mine.*

By the time Tom entered the house, Cat was in the parlour in all her tattered, smelly glory. 'I was just about to go fishin',' she said joyously, noting the sudden pallor on Tom's face when he saw her. 'Care to join in?'

Tom nodded bravely, and soon the two were tramping through the woods. Cat took the lead, splashing deliberately through streams that were muddy with spring runoff. Tom panted to keep up with her, and after nearly an hour of walking he asked, 'Ought we to go so far, Cat? You know there's Injun talk again.'

Cat paused just long enough to turn up her nose at him. 'That talk's for folks afraid of their own shadows, I expect. I haven't seen any Injuns hereabouts, have you?'

'No,' Tom replied slowly, 'but – '

'The Major's scoured Brant's Orchard clean of Injuns,' Cat replied with confidence. 'Everybody knows that.'

'Except maybe the Injuns,' Tom said.

Cat pretended not to hear him. She pushed along through the underbrush until she came to a spring-fed pool. 'Here we are,' she said cheerfully. 'Not such a bad hike, was it?' She opened the basket she'd carried over her arm and drew out fish hooks, lines, and a tin cup packed with a tangle of earthworms. She selected the pinkest, fattest worm of the bunch and held it up for Tom's admiration. 'Not bad, huh?' she asked briskly. 'I dug 'em up myself this morning. Why, these worms are so fat that if I don't catch any fish I figure the worms themselves'd make a fine dinner.'

Tom looked at her with such disappointment that Cat had to bite her lips to conceal her merriment. She bent her head and smiled to herself as she baited her hook. She had no doubt that after today she would be rid of Tom's romantic attentions.

But suddenly the hook, worm and all, went flying out of her hands. Tom grabbed her shoulders so forcefully that she stumbled against him. 'Oh, Cat!' he cried, his brown eyes shining as if he wanted to weep over the coarse thing she'd become. 'You've been around those brothers of yours so long you've almost become one of them. But when we're married, you'll have nought to do but mind our house and turn out dainty needlework!' He took her hand, grubby with dirt, and pressed it dramatically over his own heart, as if sealing a pledge.

Cat wanted to laugh. Tom was looking at her with the calflike eyes of an idiot. Any romantic notion she'd ever had of him had been driven clean out of her head by his silliness. Did all boys act like such fools when they fell in love? she wondered. If they did, she was quite certain she would never be able to love any of them.

Tom's insistent arms around her drew her back to reality. She saw that, despite her ruined buckskins and unladylike behaviour, Tom Alexander meant to kiss her. In a burst of energy, she twisted away from him and darted off through the woods, her laugh waving in the air behind her.

'Cat!' he called after her, his voice showing how much she'd strained his patience. 'Come back here, Cat!'

She heard the crackle of leaves as he started after her. Then, suddenly, the woods went silent. Cat paused on the far side of a huge old hemlock tree. When she heard Tom's voice, he sounded calm and even happy.

'All right, Cat,' he called. 'I know what you're about. You won't kiss me again 'til I've talked to your Pa proper. Well, I will! I'm on my way right now!'

Panic swept Cat from the soles of her feet to the roots of her hair. *Talk to the Major!* Tom might just be crazy enough to do it. Worse yet, the Major might just be crazy enough to say yes! Cat thought quickly. 'Wouldn't you like one more kiss first?' she sang out sweetly.

'Course I would,' Tom called back.

'Well, you can have it,' she shouted, 'soon as you catch me!' She darted from her hiding place and fled through the sun-dappled woods. Tom was no match for her swiftness, and she knew it. She hoped that by the time Tom realized the same thing he would be too exhausted to do anything but slink home.

She ran far into the woods, paying no attention to distance or direction. There would be time enough to find her way home later. And if she couldn't find her way, Ike and James would come looking for her as they always did. The important thing – the only thing that mattered – was to run the idea of marriage out of Tom Alexander's head.

Cat laced her way deep into a forest of towering

hemlocks. They were so gigantic that they cut off the sun. Shadows surrounded her as she ran. Then, suddenly, one of the shadows rose up and stopped her in her path.

She started to smile, certain that the Indian before her was one of her father's trading friends. But the fierce Shawnee bore no resemblance to anyone she had ever seen before. And when he raised his hand, Cat saw the blue flash of a steel hatchet.

Before she could take flight, a bronze hand clamped down over her shoulder. Her mouth opened, but his eyes told her not to cry out. For a moment she just stood there, the paralyzing brown hand gripping her shoulder. The hatchet swooped and circled above her head like an oddly graceful bird. She squeezed her eyes shut and clamped her jaws together, determined not to let this Indian, scarcely older than she was, see her fear.

She felt a pulling *pop* all around her head – her scalp being lifted, surely. But then her own hair came tumbling down into her face, and the Indian uttered a startled grunt.

Cat looked up, as startled as the Indian. It took her a minute to remember that she'd been wearing the fur cap. The Indian was holding it in his hatchet hand. The look on his face told Cat all she needed to know. Thinking her a boy, he'd intended to scalp her; now she was going to live because he saw that she was a girl.

She found her voice, then, and her strength. With a gasp she wrenched free of the young Indian. 'Get away!' she hissed in Shawnee.

His eyes flew open in surprise. Seeing her opportunity. Cat sprang away from him. But her strength was no match for the Indian. His legs were like steel springs, and he flashed up to grab her. Cat felt his vicelike grip on her shoulders again. She kicked uselessly as he flung her over his shoulder and carried her off through the woods.

Cat stiffled the scream that rose automatically in her throat. If she cried for help, Tom might come. Cat had already seen enough to know that the Indian would not hesitate to kill him – or any other male either. She was safe because she was a girl, but she dared not risk the lives of her kinfolk nearby.

No, there was nothing she could do but suffer the Indian to carry her away like a sack of cornmeal. She quelled the fear by reminding herself that Ike and James and the major were sure to come searching for her, trading beads and blankets and bacon to get her back. Hadn't she heard a hundred such stories? She would get back home again. She would get back home if she had to do it all by herself.

Her head and arms hung down over the Indian's naked back. Moving cautiously, Cat jerked a buckskin fringe from her sleeve and dropped it to the ground. *There*, she thought. *There's something for you to follow, James. You ought to know it, Ike – it's a piece of your own castoff buckskins. And if you don't happen to see it, I'll use it myself as a trail marker to come back by!*

Cat breathed in deeply and caught the scent of sweet woodsmoke – woodsmoke from her Pa's own smokehouse. She pictured her mother and father and brothers and the crowded, jolly little cabin that was her home. Something dangerously like a sob shook her chest. The Indian cocked his head and glanced back at her, and Cat turned the sob into a fit of coughing.

Chapter 3

The Indian carried Cat for miles into the forest. His long strides ate up the ground, and his breathing barely increased under her weight. To Cat, it seemed that an eternity passed before the Indian stopped and dumped her to the ground beside a small stream.

Cat had not had anything to eat or drink for hours. She plunged her face into the stream and drank, letting the cool water fill her empty stomach. When she looked up, she saw that the young Indian was looking at her. He waited until he had her full attention, then he clicked his tongue rapidly against his teeth and gave a low-pitched call. A magnificent horse burst from its hiding place in the woods.

The young Indian was obviously proud of the horse, for he grasped the bridle and paraded the animal back and forth in front of Cat. Then he pointed to the copper armbands circling his own biceps and nodded fiercely at her. 'Shawnee,' he said, making a sweeping gesture that included the horse as well as himself. 'Kispokotha Shawnee.'

Cat hoped her face was not turning as chalky white as she felt inside. Kispokotha Shawnee lived far to the north. Of all the branches of the Shawnee nation, they were the fiercest, the most warlike. She remembered what her brother Ike had once told her: if all the scalps taken by the Kispokotha Shawnee were piled on top of each other, there'd be a mountain of hair reaching clear to heaven.

Cat forced herself to meet the Indian's eye calmly. She set her lips in a firm line. He hadn't killed her yet, so maybe he wasn't going to. Or maybe, she thought with sick fear, he was waiting to do it when he got back to his village.

The Indian said something to Cat. She understood Shawnee, but not these tangled syllables. They rushed past her like water tumbling through a cataract. Cat suspected that the Indian spoke rapidly on purpose, hoping to confuse her. When she looked up and saw the sly smile on his face, she was sure of it.

He jerked her to her feet and spoke again, slowing down just enough for her to catch the words before they skittered off.

He wants me to 'gratulate him on what a great warrior he is, Cat realized. *Well, I hope he's not holding his breath for my praise!* It was a joke in the Brant family that whenever Cat set her mind on something, her eyes turned from blue to flint. That's the colour they were now. She had no intention of feeding the Shawnee's greedy pride. 'I reckon a real warrior wouldn't care 'bout a girl's opinion anyway,' she said sullenly, half hoping he'd understand her.

But the Indian only narrowed his black eyes at her. Again, Cat did not understand. To her, it seemed as if he was saying something like *two stars walking in the sky.* Looking at her with his dark eyes, the Shawnee pointed upward. Twilight was just beginning to fall. Cat's glance followed the movement of his arm. Pale stars glistened above the canopy of treetops. 'Stars,' Cat said in Shawnee, glad that she remembered the word.

He nodded his head triumphantly, as proud as if

he had taught her the word himself. Then he pointed again, first at one star, then at another. One star, Two stars. He paused, slapped his chest, and looked triumphantly at Cat.

Suddenly she understood. That was his name: Two Stars Walking in the Sky – Two Stars for short. Because the Indian seemed willing to go on slapping himself and pointing at the sky all night long, Cat finally gave in. 'Oh, all right,' she mumbled in English. 'I'll say your name if it'll make you happy.' She switched to Shawnee. 'Two Stars!'

To her relief, the Indian seemed satisfied. Then Cat had an idea. She drew herself up and slapped her own chest. 'Cat,' she said firmly. 'Catherine Brant.'

With an angry shake of his head, Two Stars leaped towards her. He gave her a push that sent her sprawling backward on to the ground.

As soon as Cat got her breath back, she climbed to her feet. Slowly, looking the Shawnee straight in the eye, she slapped her chest again. 'Catherine Brant,' she said again, her voice clear in the still air. '*My* name – Catherine Brant!'

But Two Stars pushed her down again. He shook his head violently at her, his black eyes clouding with anger.

Cat stared up at him. He pointed at her and unleashed a tangled flow of words. Apparently, as far as Two Stars was concerned, she was no longer Catherine Brant. Instead she was someone called Girl Who Dresses Like Boy, or Girl-Boy. She was a captive and nothing more.

It doesn't matter, Cat told herself. *It doesn't matter what he wants to call me. I've been Catherine Brant all my life until now; I'll be Catherine Brant again, soon as Ike and James and Pa find me.* She lowered her head, hunching her shoulders against the cold of the evening. *But what if they don't find me?* her mind asked. For just as she had heard stories of captives traded quickly back to their families, she'd also heard of those who lived so long with the Indians that time erased the whole white world from their minds.

The fine horse was not for Cat to ride. Warriors rode horses, Two Stars told her. Women and children and captives walked. Therefore, Girl Who Dresses Like Boy would walk. To make his point clear, he tied one end of a long sinew rope around Cat's waist. Then, holding the free end of the rope, he mounted the big grey horse and set off, leading Cat behind him like a dog on a leash.

Cat made a face at him behind his back. Warriors ride, indeed! Defiantly, she tugged another buckskin fringe loose and dropped it behind her. What kind of warrior was he, anyway? Didn't he know that if he let her walk she'd be able to leave trail marks wherever she wanted to?

For two days, Cat rationed the buckskin fringes carefully. If too many of them were missing, she knew, Two Stars would be sure to notice. Whenever she could, she marked the trail in other ways. Once, when Two Stars' horse lunged forward, Cat deliberately lagged behind. The sinew rope pulled taut, jerking her off her feet.

Two Stars stopped just long enough to let her regain her footing. He glowered at her over his shoulder, but Cat didn't mind. As she got up, she noted with satisfaction that her fall had snapped and torn the branches of a bush.

On the third day, Cat's own rumbling stomach woke her before dawn. She'd had no meat to eat since her capture, a time that seemed an eternity ago. When she tried to tell Two Stars of her need for food, he pretended not to understand the meaning of her gestures.

Cat narrowed her eyes at him. 'You know what I'm getting at, all right,' she accused. 'I'm hungry. *Hungry*!'

Two Stars paid no more attention to her than the rocks and trees did. Instead, he mounted his big grey horse. There was nothing Cat could do but set her jaw and trudge along behind him.

That afternoon they came to a wide, deep river. Cat's heart sank at the sight of it, for its swift, tumbling waters were sure to erase any footprints she managed to leave behind.

Two Stars pulled Cat up on to the horse for the crossing. She clung to the animal's mane and tried not to shiver as the icy water rose to cover her legs. It was early April, and the river was swollen with the runoff of melted mountain snow. To Cat, hungry and exhausted, the swirling current felt like a torrent of fluid ice. She hoped that Two Stars, mounted behind her, couldn't feel the tremors that shook her body.

As soon as they reached the far bank, Two Stars signalled for Cat to get off the horse. Cat, seeing her chance to mark their crossing, pretended not to understand him. When she didn't slide down by herself, Two Stars gave her an impatient shove. Cat spun away from the horse, losing her footing on the uneven ground. Shielding her hand from Two Stars' view, she grasped a seedling elm and jerked it up by the roots. *There*, she thought, pushing herself to her feet. *That ought to help Ike and James.*

But when Two Stars turned to look back at her, his glance fell on the uprooted seedling. His dark eyes flashed with sudden understanding. He leaped off the horse, shouting at Cat and making threatening gestures at her.

Cold fear swept through Cat, but she stood her ground. She looked down at her feet, pretending not to notice when Two Stars picked up the seedling and hurled it toward the river. Out of the corner of her eye, she saw the current catch it and carry it away.

Still shouting, Two Stars grasped Cat by the elbow and drove her back toward the river. He made her stand in ankle-deep water, holding the horse's bridle, while he covered their tracks with earth and leaves. Then he mounted the horse, pulled Cat roughly up in front of him, and set off downstream.

Tears of defeat welled in Cat's eyes, but she shook them away. Even if she'd lost her chance to mark the trail, at least she was riding now. And that was just as well, she told herself, for she was so tired and hungry she couldn't have walked another step.

Cat awoke with a jolt. Her hands and feet were tied, but that wasn't why she woke up. Two Stars tied her hands and feet every night, and she had grown used to that. But something was different.

Cat inched herself to a sitting position. Two Stars was gone! She blinked against the harsh morning sunlight. The big grey horse was gone too. Her heart began to flutter with wild excitement. If only she could free herself, she could run away. She could start back on the long trail that would take her home.

Her mind raced ahead of her body, picturing each part of the journey. The hard part would be getting back to the big river, the one they had crossed two days ago. Ever since that crossing. Two Stars had been careful to cover their trail. Cat would have to rely on memory and instinct to find the river again.

She would find the river, she assured herself. And once she crossed it, she would be as good as home. For on the other side of the river lay all the trail marks she had left behind. And somewhere too, on the other side of the river, her father and brothers were looking for her.

But even before she looked for the river, she would have to look for something to eat. In all the days since her capture, she had had only a few handfuls of berries to eat. Unless she found something more substantial, she would not have the strength to across the river.

Cat chafed against the sinews that bound her hands. After half an hour's steady work, she jerked one hand free. She was just leaning down to unbind her ankles when something came crashing through the woods at her.

Her heart sank when she looked up and saw Two Stars riding toward her on the horse. There was no chance of escaping now, and her visions of home fell away in the bright sunlight. Still, she'd almost got away. She knew it was possible now, and she knew she would try again.

Cat slipped her hand back into the sinew bands.

For the first time, she noticed that Two Stars was grinning. Wherever he had been, he was enormously pleased with himself. He held a dead rabbit up for her to admire. Then he hopped off the horse and began to untie her.

'Girl-Boy cook food,' he said commandingly.

Cat nodded. Her mouth watered at the sight of the rabbit. Food – real food! 'Yes, yes,' she said quickly. 'Girl-Boy cook.'

Two Stars grinned approvingly. He leaned back against a tree and watched her clean and spit the rabbit.

Sudden annoyance seized Cat. 'One rabbit all?' she asked. She'd been hungry for days, and one rabbit didn't seem nearly enough. She thought of the way her brothers made the woods yield deer and squirrel and tasty possum. Two Stars had no right at all to look as pleased as he did. 'Next time, Girl-Boy hunt,' she said.

Cat half expected him to rise up and hit her, but he didn't. Instead, a look of sheepish chagrin crossed his face. And Cat could have sworn that underneath his coppery skin she saw blush of embarrassment. That blush, and the smell of sizzling rabbit, made her feel better.

Cat heard the noises of Two Stars' village long before they came within sight of it. The barking of dogs and the cries of children filled the air. Hazy smoke drifted through the treetops, pungent with the aroma of cooking food.

To Cat, the smells and the noises were achingly familiar. Home sounds were home sounds, no matter whom they belonged to. The sweet, tempting smoke only reminded her how far from her own home she was. They'd travelled for over a week, and Cat knew she was at least a hundred miles from home.

Although Two Stars had allowed Cat to share the horse with him since the day they'd crossed the big river, he made her walk into the village. Cat sniffed at this show of pride. No doubt he wanted to play the warrior's part, leading his humble captive triumphantly into his village.

Well enough, Cat thought, but she knew how much of a great warrior Two Stars really was. During the last days of the journey, it had been Cat's skill with a slingshot that had kept him fed.

Cat's spine stiffened as they approached the ring of bark lodges. She'd been putting off this moment in her mind, though she'd known it would come. The cold and discomfort of the trail were known enemies, but what new enemies would she face here?

Children danced out towards them, calling and shouting. They put their hands up and touched Cat's fine, tawny-coloured hair with their fingers. They thrust their faces into hers, gazing up into her sky-blue eyes. Cat did her best to ignore them, pushing them gently aside, but they blocked her way completely. She walked cautiously, eyes downcast, for she realized that her whole future – and perhaps even her life – was at stake.

Lured by the children's cries, adults also cast aside their work. Women left the hides they had been scraping clean – Cat recognized the fleshing knives some still held in their hands. A pretty young woman, balancing a basket of dandelion greens on her hip, giggled at the sight of Cat's man-style buckskins. She fell silent when the handsome young man who was probably her husband shot her a stern glance.

Other men appeared also, though the women far outnumbered them. Cat decided that many of the men must be away from the village, hunting or trading or making war. Well enough, she thought. It would make escaping all the easier when the time came.

Cat longed to stare at them – at all of them – just as they stared at her. But she couldn't risk it. So whatever she observed, she observed through downcast eyes. One tall young man looked on with particular interest. 'So,' he said, his wide mouth wrinkling in a sarcastic grimace. 'My little brother returns from his great hunting trip.'

'I don't see any deer,' another man said, and laughter rippled through the group.

'Perhaps he got something else by mistake,' the man who was Two Stars' older brother said.

Without replying, Two Stars slid off the grey horse. He ignored the jest of his brother and sought the attention of another man – a man dressed so splendidly that Cat knew he must be a chief. 'Two Stars returns,' he said.

The chief was standing beside a man with long white hair and a face so wrinkled it looked like a dried apple. Cat believed he must be a chief too, for it was he who spoke to Two Stars.

'Two Stars was sent away to learn to hunt,' the old man said. 'Because Two Stars no longer has a father to guide him, I, Swift River, decided this should be so. Two Stars is past the age of learning this thing! All Shawnee men hunt, but Two Stars perhaps believes that meat falls from the skies!'

Cat pressed her lips together to keep from joining in the laughter this remark caused. The younger chief, who name was Spotted Bird, now stepped forward. 'Two Stars is gone far longer than necessary,' he said firmly. 'His mother worries about him. His older brother, Running Calf, must hunt meat for the lodge. And now that Two Stars returns, does he return with meat?'

'I do not see any meat,' Swift River said. 'I see nothing but a pale ghost following behind Two Stars.' With a jerk of his chin the old man looked away, as if disgusted with the whole topic.

Two Stars lifted his chin. 'What Swift River and Spotted Bird see is a captive – a captive I took in the village of the whites! Surrounded by enemies, *I* took her!' Two Stars' chest swelled with pride. Cat wanted to walk right up to him and punch him. *Surrounded by enemies, my eye!* she thought angrily. *If Pa or Ike or James had been anywhere near, he'd never have laid a hand on me!*

Through the lashes of her lowered eyelids, Cat saw the two chiefs of the village exchange glances. 'And what does Two Stars intend to do with the captive?' Spotted Bird asked.

Two Stars drew himself up. Cat saw the muscles of his back and shoulders flex. Suddenly she was listening hard, grateful that she knew enough Shawnee to understand her fate. 'She is my captive,' Two Stars said imperiously. 'So she will be my women. *My* woman!' he repeated.

Cat shivered. She waited for Swift River or Spotted Bird to speak – to say that the white captive would *not* be his woman. But the two men were silent, and after a moment Two Stars turned to lead her away. A crushing weight filled Cat's chest. She was his woman. Until she escaped.

Chapter 4

Night sky showed through the split ceiling of the bark lodge. In claiming Cat as his woman. Two Stars had forgotten that he had no home of his own. Until now, he'd lived with his mother in a snug, tidy lodge next to the lodge of his brother, Running Calf.

But when Two Stars directed Cat to his mother's lodge, they found the older woman firmly barring the way. She would gladly welcome a daughter-in-law courted, won, and married in the proper way, she said. But if Two Stars wanted a lazy man's marriage, she would not welcome him. He no longer had a place inside her lodge.

There was an abandoned lodge on the edge of the village, and that was where Cat and Two Stars ended up. 'You make this home,' he commanded, dropping in a heap the two blankets his mother had agreed to give them. Then he disappeared.

Cat looked around. There were so many holes in the roof that dusky light sifted down, showing her the weeds that sprouted up through the dirt floor. Scattered about were a few baskets, a kettle, bowls made from split gourds, and two spoons made from horns. It would take a lot of homemaking, Cat thought, to turn the place into anything even remotely homey.

She used the last of the afternoon light to weed her floor. When dusk fell and Two Stars still had not returned, she decided she would have to see about getting a fire herself. She went to her nearest neighbour – a young couple with children – and asked for light. When the young woman invited her into the lodge, the sight of a true home made Cat feel lonelier and more miserable than ever.

The young woman's husband sat near the fire, squinting slightly as he attached a metal tip to a long, straight arrow. He talked as he worked, telling his wide-eyed son a story about hunting for brown bears. A little girl sat nearby, stitching moccasins with thick fur lining. 'Was it this bear, Father?' she asked, holding up one of the moccasins. Her father nodded and went on with his story.

Cat would gladly have curled up by their fire and spent the rest of the night there, but soon the young wife handed her a stone bowl filled with dry moss. The bowl was warm, and embers glowed in the nest of moss. Cat had no choice but to thank the woman for her kindness and return to her own cold, lonely little hut.

Two Stars still had not returned, so Cat built a fire and snuggled down beside it, wrapping herself in one of the two blankets Two Stars' mother had given them. She fell asleep gazing up through a great hole in the roof, counting the stars and wondering if Ike, James, and her father were somewhere close, looking up and counting the same stars.

The first thing she felt was pressure against her chest. Her eyes flew open, and before she could cry out a hand covered her mouth. In the dying light of the fire she saw Two Stars' face. He was smiling, and the pressure on her chest was his body pressing against hers.

Without pausing to consider the consequences, she bit down on his hand – hard. He jerked it away with a yelp loud enough to wake the whole village. 'What do you think you're doing?' she hissed. She would have used stronger language, but she didn't know any Shawnee swear words.

Two Stars grappled for her wrists. Cat gasped at his strength. In spite of her frantic efforts, he managed to pin her down. 'You're my woman,' he said, his chest heaving against hers.

Cat worked a leg free and kicked him. Startled, Two Stars loosened his grip. Cat slithered out from underneath him. He retaliated by grabbing her ankle, but it was too late – she snatched a glowing stick from the fire and brandished it at him.

'You let go of me,' she said. *'Now!'* Her voice was shrill with fear and fury.

Two Stars let go of her ankle. His face showed that the matter was far from settled. 'You're my woman,' he said firmly.

Cat set her jaw. 'Not that way, I'm not your woman,' she said, her voice as firm as his. Keeping the ember between herself and Two Stars like a shield, she crawled back to her bed. 'This is my bed, my blanket,' she told him. 'Your blanket's over there.'

For a long moment the two stared at each other. Then, with a grunt, Two Stars picked up his blanket and left the hut. Cat learned later that he spent the night huddled among the ponies. No doubt he'd meant to wake early and sneak back to the lodge, but instead he slept late and was discovered. The story of how Two Stars' woman refused to be his woman was told all over the village. It was a source of much laughter, and everyone seemed to believe that Two Stars had got exactly what he deserved.

Inside the lodge, Cat shook with anger. In spite of the fire and in spite of the blanket wrapped around her, she was cold. Fear ran through her veins like ice water. How many more times would this happen? And how many more times would she be able to put Two Stars off?

Cat sat by the lodge fire, her head bent low as she attached a stretchy piece of rabbit gut to the prongs of a Y-shaped piece of wood. The smell of roasting venison filled the air, making it hard for her to concentrate on her work. Cat's mouth watered, and she licked her lips. 'Moving Shadow has been hunting again,' she said accusingly, glaring at Two Stars. 'How fortunate his wife and children are, to have such a fine hunter in their lodge.'

She had grown bolder since her first night in the lodge. Two Stars had not approached her again. In fact, he seemed to avoid her as much as possible. Perhaps he realized the great mistake he'd made in making her his woman.

Now he lay on his blankets pretending to be a great warrior. He was also pretending to be deaf, a habit that Cat found infuriating. She sniffed the air again, her hunger growing with every breath. She had been in the Shawnee village over a week. In all that time Two Stars had added meat to their stewpot only once. 'You're the sorriest hunter I've ever seen,' Cat muttered sullenly.

Without a word, Two Stars rose and left the hut.

Anger, kindled by hunger, seized Cat. Without dropping the Y-shaped stick in her hand, she jumped to her feet and followed Two Stars out into the sunlight. 'Stop pretendin' you can't hear me!' she shouted in English. A group of women weaving baskets under a shady tree looked up at her with open mouths. Cat didn't even notice them. 'You don't do anything all day long – least you can do is learn to hunt. I'm tired of livin' on nothin' but onions and dried pumpkins! Maybe you can't hunt worth a lick, but I can – *and I'm going to!*'

Swift River came out of his lodge to see who was disturbing the peace of his village. Too late, Cat realized what she'd done. She'd lost her temper and done what no Shawnee woman would think of doing: she'd carried a lodge fight out into the square for everyone to hear. Everyone within earshot had dropped their work and come running. Now she stood in front of them like a madwoman, holding the homemade slingshot in her hand like a club.

Cat had no idea what would happen next. She half expected them to rush up to grab her, as if she were a dangerous animal. What was the punishment for what she'd done? Whipping? Branding? Her mind ran wild with hideous possibilities. Whatever it was, it was sure to be better than starving to death, which was what she was doing with Two Stars.

Everyone – even Two Stars – was staring at her expectantly. With a flicker of relief, Cat saw that their eyes were full of curiosity. She'd shouted such a bubbling stew of English words that she'd half hypnotized them!

Cautiously, she pointed to Two Stars. 'No hunt,'

she explained in Shawnee. A murmur of agreement swept the circle. 'No hunt,' Cat repeated, her voice stronger than before. Two Stars looked as if he'd like to take flight. Cat rubbed her flat palm against her stomach. 'I am hungry,' she said.

Cat's mind raced ahead, trying to put her thoughts into Shawnee. 'When I smell the meat cooking in the lodge of Moving Shadow, I . . . I . . .' She paused. She didn't know the Shawnee way of saying that one had gone momentarily crazy. Perhaps Shawnee never went crazy. Finally, Cat struck her hands together and shook her head, hoping the Shawnee would understand how the smell of the roasting venison had driven her to the breaking point.

They did. A ripple of laughter shook the crowd. The tight, uncertain feeling in Cat's chest began to ease. 'Since Two Stars will not hunt, I will hunt myself,' she said, holding the slingshot up for all to see. '*I* will hunt!'

They did not cheer, as white people might have done, but Cat felt their approval nonetheless. Gripping her slingshot, she turned and walked toward the path that led to the hunting forests. No one stopped her, and those who stood in her way moved aside to let her pass. Cat's heart leaped up in triumph. She was free to hunt. Soon she would be free altogether.

Cat hunted so successfully that no one questioned her comings or goings. Even Two Stars, glad to have a full stewpot to enjoy, paid little attention to her absences. Cat saw that the door to freedom lay open before her. All she had to do was walk through it.

She made her preparations carefully, drying bits of fresh meat and hiding them in her deerskin hunting pouch. She no longer wore her buckskins but dressed in the long fringed shift worn by all Shawnee women. Now she rolled her old shirt and britches into a tight ball and packed them into the hunting pouch as well. She even managed to trade four fine fat squirrels for a sharp new knife, saying she needed it to skin game with.

Cat made her escape on a day of stormy weather. She forced herself to walk slowly out of the village, as she always did when going hunting. Once safely out of sight, however, she broke into a broad grin. She knew how fond of comfort Two Stars was. He would doze all night by the fire, hoping for her return, rather than search for her in the raw, rainy night.

She turned south, for she had already determined that south was where the big river was. Once she found it, she would follow it east to the place where she and Two Stars had made their crossing. Then she would cross it and follow her own trail marks back to Brant's Orchard.

Brant's Orchard – home! She hadn't dared to think of it until now. Her feet quickened, and her heart sent blood pulsing through her veins. She tried to imagine the looks on the faces of her father, mother, and brothers when she appeared in the doorway of their cabin. Or perhaps she wouldn't meet them in the cabin at all – perhaps she would find them somewhere on the trail, searching for her as she was searching for them.

The thought of home carried Cat for miles. She walked swiftly through the drizzling rain, pausing only once to drink from a stream. When she grew hungry in the late afternoon, she chewed on the dried meat she had brought with her. She did not trust herself to build a fire – not yet. She was still too close to the Shawnee village for that.

Just before sunset, Cat heard a sound that raised the hairs on the back of her neck. Branches snapped and rustled, as if an enormous beast were moving through the forest. For a minute she stood stiff and still. Her hand slid toward the knife that dangled from her belt. Then, before she could dart away, the beast crashed through the gloom and stood directly before her.

Cat saw them – three Indians on horseback – come clear of the shadows. They were silent and majestic as ghosts, looking down at her with narrow eyes and stern faces.

Cat's heart thudded in her throat, loud as a bell ringing her to wakefulness. She turned to flee, but before she had taken two steps one of the Indians, swift as a shadow, swooped down after her. He grasped her firmly by the arms, lifting her up so easily that her feet dangled in the air. He carried her to the tallest of the Indians and set her down before his horse.

His face was commanding, with a firm, hawklike nose and broad cheekbones. A headdress of red porcupine quills rose like a crown from the top of his head. Cat looked up at him, and their eyes met. In that second, she saw him read everything about her – her captivity, her attempt to escape. But he spoke to her as if he understood nothing at all, keeping all his knowledge behind his eyes. 'Shawnee?' he asked her.

Cat nodded. The other Indians looked on silently. It was clear that this tall man in the red headdress was their chief.

He was looking down at her again. 'Lost perhaps?' he asked.

Cat shook her head. She could not tell him the truth about what she'd been doing, even if he already knew. 'Hunting,' she explained.

The Indian's eyes widened in amusement. 'Hunting?' he repeated. 'Hunting with no weapon?'

Cat pointed to the hunting pouch slung over her shoulder. 'In here,' she said.

The chief's teeth flashed white in the drizzly gloom of the forest. 'Must be very fast,' he chuckled. The other Indians laughed with him.

That was the end of the interview. Cat was bundled on to a horse behind one of the warriors and taken back to the village she'd just escaped from.

Spotted Bird and Swift River were glad to welcome Blackfish to their village. But their eyebrows lifted in mild surprise when they saw that Cat was with him. In swift Shawnee, Blackfish explained how they had found her in the woods. He did not need to tell them she'd been trying to escape – they figured that out for themselves.

Then the voices of the men went low, and Cat realized that they must be telling Blackfish about her life with Two Stars. Cat saw Blackfish throw his head back and laugh – a gesture that reminded her of her father.

Cat was brought into the council lodge, and Two Stars was sent for.

'Our Shawnee friend Blackfish has found something of yours,' Spotted Bird said.

'What?' Two Stars asked sleepily, blinking in the smoky firelight. It was late night, and the young man had been pulled from a sound slumber. In spite of everything, Cat found room in her heart to enjoy his confusion.

'Have you missed something?' Swift River asked, amusement dancing in his old eyes.

Two Stars looked uncomfortable. 'Perhaps Swift River will explain his meaning to me,' he ventured.

Blackfish, too, joined in the game. 'Has he not missed the hunter from his lodge?' he asked, stepping aside to reveal Cat. 'Surely she was not trying to escape,' he went on, 'although it looked very much that way.'

Two Stars shot Cat a murderous glance, as if he wished for all the world that she really had escaped. She saw him struggle to invent a face-saving story. 'Yes, I send her to hunt meat,' Two Stars said. 'I tell her to come back only when she has meat. She does not find meat today, so she does not return today. It is of no concern to me.'

The three older men exchanged glances. Blackfish stepped in and kept the ball rolling. 'She is a good hunter then?'

Two Stars brightened. 'Yes, a good hunter. A good captive in every way, worth many horses.'

Blackfish was silent for a moment. 'Too bad I have no extra horses with me,' he said deliberately. 'I would give much for someone so valuable.'

Two Stars smiled greedily. 'Silver is worth more than horses,' he said.

Blackfish's eyes slid subtly and sadly down to the two silver cuffs he wore on his wrists. 'I have only a little silver with me,' he said.

Two Stars' eyes were on the splendid cuffs. They were of German silver, heavily engraved and beautiful in spite of their tarnish. 'I will consider it,' he said, barely able to contain himself; and after a too brief pause he added, 'Done.'

Cat was in shock. That morning she'd belonged to Two Stars. In the afternoon she'd escaped and, for a few brief, wonderful hours, belonged to no one but herself. Now she belonged to someone again. She'd been sold to Blackfish for the pair of silver cuffs.

The world was spinning too fast for her, and her exhausted heart could hardly keep up with it. The problem was, no one asked her whether she could keep up or not. Two days later, when Blackfish and his warriors left the village, she was packed along with them like a piece of pottery or an extra blanket.

Two Stars did not come out to see them off, and Cat did not grieve over her leaving. No matter where she was going, she thought, it would be an improvement over the broken-down hut she shared with Two Stars. Besides, there was something about Blackfish that she liked. Perhaps it was the way the other men looked to him with respect, or perhaps it was the wry, humorous way he spoke. 'We are glad to have Two Stars' woman with us,' he told her, a faint, curious smile lighting the corners of his mouth.

Cat felt her cheeks redden. 'I was not Two Stars' woman. Not the important way.'

Blackfish nodded, showing that he believed her. Once again, Cat was no one's woman. Maybe she would never be anyone's woman; maybe she would miss the simple miracle of love. Or maybe love was waiting for her on the tangled paths ahead, crouching in the shadows, ready to leap into her heart without warning.

Chapter 5

They lost the mountains as they went north, Cat felt the anchor that tied her to home loosening. She was drifting, uncertain of her place and even, at times, of who she was. The quick sureness went out of her, and the fiery temper she'd shown to Two Stars evaporated. Instead there arose a stubborn, plodding will to survive.

The Indians led her farther and farther from Brant's Orchard. The familiar, sheltering foothills that had been her guideposts vanished. One day Cat looked around and realized that if Blackfish were to set her free she would not know which way to go.

In place of the foothills lay broad, gentle hills – hills that rose and curved in an endless procession, like ocean waves. One hill looked exactly like another to Cat, and the forest she moved through today looked no different to her from the forest she had passed through yesterday.

Sometimes the forests broke apart, showing meadows that ran like sea foam towards the horizon. Spring grass, tender and feathery, reached up to brush the horses' forelegs. There were wildflowers, too, showing between the wands of grass.

A field of yellow dandelions, orange hawkweed, and purple-blue asters reminded Cat of a quilt she and her mother had been working on. The pattern, called 'Garden Path', was difficult because the pieces were six-sided. Cat remembered how easily her mother had sewn them, while she herself had pricked her fingers and sighed over her crooked stitches. Suddenly, tears flooded her eyes, and the bright field blurred in front of her. She had to bite her lip hard to keep from crying, and the quizzical look Blackfish gave her made her think that somehow he guessed her homesickness.

Going from the open, sunshine-filled meadows back into the forests was like being plunged to the bottom of a cool, dark well. It always took Cat's eyes a few minutes to adjust to the dimness. One day, riding behind the Indian called Sun Turns Red, she blinked up to see two fierce yellow eyes looking back at her.

Cat stiffened and uttered a cry of warning, but Blackfish and the others had already seen what she saw: directly in front of them, on the low branch of a tree, a huge cougar crouched. His ears were laid back in warning, and the muscles of his powerful shoulders twitched and quivered beneath his tawny fur.

The horses snorted fitfully, and Cat's heart throbbed with fear. To turn and retreat would invite pursuit, but to advance on the crouching animal would be even more dangerous. Cat doubted that any of the Indians – even Blackfish himself – could raise his bow and arrow before the animal flashed down upon them.

'I will talk to him,' Cat heard one of the Indians – Panther Walks – say. She couldn't believe her ears. Panther Walks had apparently lost his mind. Why else would he suggest anything so impossible?

Cat glanced at Blackfish and saw struggle in his

eyes. Swiftly, he hid his emotions. Cat saw him nod, sending the foolish young Shawnee to certain death.

Panther Walks didn't seem to move, but somehow he was off his horse and advancing toward the huge cat. The woods were still. Cat couldn't even hear her own breathing. The only sounds were the deep, purring vibrations that came from the big cat's throat.

Cat expected the cougar to attack at any moment, and she half closed her eyes to miss the horrible sight of ripped flesh and spurting blood. But seconds passed and nothing happened. When she opened her eyes wide again, she saw the cat staring down at Panther Walks, almost directly below him.

'Let us pass, brother cat,' Panther Walks said, his voice gentle in the sweet air of mid-afternoon. The Shawnee brave moved again without seeming to move at all. Cat, like the cougar, was hypnotized by his actions. 'We do not harm your forest or your children. Today is not the day we seek your claws and hide.'

The yellow eyes blinked with lazy curiosity. Panther Walks waited, his eyes never leaving the cat. After a few minutes, the cougar raised one huge front paw and, with surpreme indifference, began to lick the pads of his foot. His tongue, pink and innocent as a house-cat's, lolled between sharp, daggerlike teeth. After he finished washing, he looked again at Panther Walks. Then, with a final, dismissing glance, he rose and stretched. He melted so quickly into the forest that he seemed to vanish.

Cat let out a long sigh of relief. Her chest ached, and she realized she'd been breathing in short, shallow gasps. Sun Turns Red turned back to look at her, his mouth flexing just enough to suggest a smile. What had just happened seemed like a dream to her, and he caught the confusion in her eyes.

Later, when the two of them were off pulling up wild onions for dinner, Sun Turns Red took her confusion away. He explained that when a person is named after a certain kind of animal, that person has special understanding with the animal. Often, the person becomes like the animal of his name. Cat thought of Panther Walks, of his hypnotic way of walking and the way his movements could be quick and sudden. She nodded, showing Sun Turns Red that she understood.

'It is because of this understanding that Panther Walks asked his father's permission to speak to his brother cat.'

His father's permission! Cat understood, suddenly, the conflict she had seen in Blackfish's eyes. Panther Walks was his son, and, though he had not wanted to deny his son's request, he had been full of concern for him. As Cat absorbed this new information, she found herself respecting Blackfish more than ever. In the same situation, she thought, her own father would have behaved in much the same way. Another wave of homesickness washed over her.

'You don't have an animal name,' she pointed out to cover her emotions. 'Neither did Two Stars.'

'Often a person is named for an omen,' Sun Turns Red explained. 'I was born on a day when haze rose to hide the brightness of the sun, and so I was named Sun Turns Red. Then, too, a name is often changed – when a person achieves something new or if the old name is unlucky. Tecumseh is one such.'

Cat shook her head. 'Tecumseh?' She did not understand, as she did now with most Shawnee names, what *Tecumseh* meant.

Sun Turns Red misunderstood her confusion. 'You will meet him,' he said. 'He is the finest of us all.'

Cat thought. 'Are girls named for animals, too?'

Sun Turns Red nodded. 'But not for panthers and bears,' he added with a chuckle. 'Girls are given names like Rabbit Feeds Her Young and Meadowlark Sings Quietly.'

'Figures,' Cat muttered in English.

'What?' Sun Turns Red asked.

Cat couldn't explain it to him, but her mind was full of comparisons. She'd thought that the Shawnee were strange and different – different by miles from her own people. But now she realized that they weren't different at all. The Shawnee world, like the world of Brant's Orchard, was a place where boys had all the chances for adventure and excitement. Girls stayed home and ended up with names like Turtle Goes Slowly and Pleasant Meadow Grass. Probably, there was even a Shawnee version of needlework and quilt-making.

Cat sighed. 'I'd like a name like Wins Many Contests or Swift Hunter,' she said, setting her jaw into its familiar jut.

Sun Turns Red laughed, but all the while he was shaking his head firmly from side to side. No, the gesture said, it wasn't possible for girls to have such adventures. It was only possible for a girl to do what she was told to do.

We'll see about that, Cat thought to herself. If Sun Turns Red had chanced to look at her at that moment, he would have seen her eyes had turned a flinty greyish-blue.

Travelling with Blackfish and the two Shawnee was nothing like travelling with Two Stars, Cat thought. For one thing, the men wwere excellent hunters and her stomach was always full.

But there was something more than that – Cat *trusted* Blackfish and his men. They were not braggarts, like Two Stars; they never spoke of the many things they knew. They did not need to. Every day Cat saw proof of it. When she lay down at night, she fell into a deep sleep, confident that Blackfish would keep danger away.

Her only sadness was the knowledge that the Indians were leading her farther and farther from home. It was a sadness so large that she couldn't bear it, and she got into the habit of jamming it down with thoughts and assurances. She would still go home, she told herself firmly. She would still see her parents and her brothers again. The difference now as that she no longer knew *how* she would go home – or when.

The days ran together like melting butter. Cat had no idea how long they'd been travelling when, suddenly, they reached their destination.

Long before they reached the village – a vast swarm of lodges – they came upon an open meadow. It happened, Cat thought, almost by accident. One moment they'd been riding through a forest of new-leafed trees. The next moment they stood at the edge of a sheer cliff, looking down on a huge sweep of meadow.

The meadow wasn't empty. Cat found her pulse

quickening at the sound of so many human voices. She slid down from her place behind Sun Turns Red and ran to the edge of the cliff. What she saw would change the path of her entire life, though she didn't know it then.

At the far end of the vast meadow, young men clustered, their dark heads and bare shoulders showing above the backs of their spotted ponies. Suddenly, a brown and grey pony burst from the group, racing north to south. The pony's mane and tail unfolded, stiff flags in the sunlight.

Cat gasped. The pony looked riderless, but now a dark shape separated itself from the streaming mane. A Shawnee brave sat up straight, his shoulders high above the pony's ears. Silver discs were tied in his hair. They caught the sun and sent it winking up at Cat.

'Tecumseh,' Sun Turns Red said behind her. 'That's Tecumseh.'

As Cat watched, the brave called Tecumseh rose and steadied himself on the back of the galloping horse. He balanced lightly on the balls of his feet, using his arms for balance.

The pony turned in a wide arc at the southern end of the meadow. Tecumseh leaned gracefully inward, never once losing his balance. When he returned to his companions, he hopped lightly down from the back of the pony.

Tecumseh, Cat saw, was taller than his companions – and older, at least a year older as far as Cat could tell. And even from this distance she could see the admiration he received from the other young men.

But then, while she was watching, another young

man rode out across the meadow. Although he must have been a year younger than Tecumseh, he was nearly as tall. His long legs gripped the pony's sides, and, as the horse gathered speed, the fringes of his red waist sash rippled in the wind. He galloped to the south end of the meadow, turned the pony, and signalled to Tecumseh and the others. Cat saw that he meant to do – or try to do – what Tecumseh had done.

Fearful for him, Cat bit her lip. But far below, in the open meadow, the young Shawnee was rising on the pony's back. He'd almost gained his footing when, suddenly, the pony jogged to miss a gopher hole.

Cat sucked in her breath. The Shawnee toppled sideways, gripping the pony's mane as he fell. Letting go, sprawling on the soft new grass, would have been easy. But the Shawnee didn't let go. He dug his fingers deep into the pony's mane and hung on.

The pony raced along, dragging the young brave, its hooves pounding so close to his face and body that Cat wanted to turn away. But she didn't. She was hypnotized by what was happening, just as the cougar had been hypnotized by the voice of Panther Walks.

From the edge of the cliff, Cat saw the Shawnee's arm and shoulder muscles working to pull himself up. The sun glimmered on his bronzed skin, and Cat felt sweat beading on her own forehead as if she were struggling with him.

A cry of excitement bubbled from her throat when the Shawnee managed to swing his leg across the pony's back. He hauled himself up on to the pony, and Cat breathed with relief to see him free of danger. Then, without pausing, he began to rise again. He planted the soles of his feet on the pony's back and flexed his knees until he stood tall and straight on the galloping pony.

Cat saw the red of his fringed sash and the gleam of his copper armbands. His head was back, and a whooping cry of triumph echoed from his throat. The other Indians cheered, Tecumseh loudest of all.

Cat's heart burst open like a flower, and wild joy blossomed in her veins. The young Shawnee, encouraged by his friends, was riding around and around the great meadow. Her eyes never left his face, and she squinted until she was dizzy, trying to make out the set of his eyes and the slope of his nose. She'd never felt quite like this before, not even at home. The feeling was so new to her, so strange, that she didn't even think to name it. She only knew that the sun had moved aside, making room for him.

A horse snorted impatiently behind her, and Cat became aware of the others again. She turned and saw that Blackfish was also looking down on the meadow. He was smiling broadly into the sunlight. 'My sons,' he said with a majestic sweep of his arm.

Lightning seemed to flash in the summer air. Blackfish's son! The boy who'd caught her heart with his wild bravery was Blackfish's son! And she, owned by Blackfish, would live in the same lodge with him!

Dazed, she walked back to the horses. Sun Turns Red offered a hand to swing her up behind him. 'Much bravery,' he said. 'Tecumseh and Blue Quail both.'

'Who?' Cat asked, hoping her voice didn't sound as quivery as she felt inside.

'Blue Quail,' Sun Turns Red repeated, although the name was already written on Cat's heart.

Chapter 6

'Why can't I live in Blackfish's lodge?' Cat asked Lark Sings at Dawn in a voice of undisguised disappointment. Lark Sings at Dawn, whom everyone called simply Lark Sings, was Blackfish's younger sister.

'There are too many boys at that lodge,' Lark Sings answered with a rueful smile. 'Boys your own age. That is why you were sent here instead. One girl in a house of boys brings trouble.'

'*I* wouldn't bring trouble,' Cat protested. 'I wouldn't be the only woman, either.' Deliberately, she used the Shawnee word for *woman* instead of *girl*. Lark Sings appeared not to notice the change of words, for she continued to use the word for *girl*.

'Oh,' Lark Sings asked, lifting her delicate eyebrows. 'You would not be the only girl?' The corners of her mouth turned up in amusement. 'How do you know that?'

'Because,' Cat reasoned, 'if Blackfish has many sons, he must also have a wife.' She raised her chin triumphantly. 'So I would not be the only woman in the lodge.'

'Blackfish's woman died many years ago,' Lark Sings told her.

Cat had no ready reply. 'Perhaps a woman's touch is needed,' she suggested.

Lark Sings laughed. 'Shawnee people are no different from your people. So many boys and just one girl – trouble, trouble, trouble.' She clicked her tongue against her teeth so meaningfully that Cat wondered if somehow she was capable of reading minds. It was just that kind of trouble that Cat was hoping for.

Cat looked away from the bright, inquiring eyes of Lark Sings. Her feelings for Blue Quail were so new that she didn't know what to do with them. Certainly she wasn't ready to share them with anyone. Yet, in spite of her urge for secrecy, her mind was bursting with questions. She tried a sideways path, asking, 'How many sons does Blackfish have?'

Lark Sings looked up from her work. She began to count on her fingers, lost track, and laughed. 'Many,' she said. 'Many sons.'

Cat tried to make her voice casual. 'In the meadow today, we saw two sons riding, Tecumseh and – and another.'

Lark Sings smiled. 'Blue Quail perhaps? He is Tecumseh's shadow.'

Cat's mouth opened in protest. In her mind, Blue Quail was no one's shadow. She caught herself in time, however, and said simply, 'Yes, Blue Quail. We saw Tecumseh and Blue Quail riding in the meadow.'

Lark Sings nodded. 'Tecumseh and Blue Quail are two of the boys in the lodge. Also there are Talks Little and Black Shoulder, Loud Voice and Panther Walks. Perhaps some others also.'

Cat looked at her quizzically. How could she be so casual – so uncertain – about how many sons were in her own brother's lodge? Without doubt, the

Shawnee people *weren't* exactly like Cat's people, no matter what Lark Sings said.

Lark Sings held up a deerskin dress spangled with fringes and small beads. 'Do you like this?' she asked. Cat nodded. The dress was lovely. Lark Sings smiled broadly. 'It shall be yours, then. You shall wear it tonight.'

'Tonight?' Cat questioned.

'At the banquet to celebrate the return of my brother. Everyone will be there.'

Everyone? Cat's eyes grew bright. Her thoughts raced away like unruly colts. In her mind she saw again the wide, sunny meadow. She saw Blue Quail standing on the pony's back, racing around and around the vast circle, outdoing even Tecumseh in the end. Her heart danced. Blue Quail would be at the banquet, and she would see him – not from a distance but face to face.

Lark Sings began unbraiding Cat's hair, working through the tangles and spreading the strands like flax between her fingers. 'A beautiful colour,' Lark Sings said.

'*Niawe*,' Cat answered automatically. 'I thank you.'

Lark Sings smoothed Cat's hair with her fingertips. 'We will wash this now,' she said gently. 'Your hair is of great beauty when not full of tangles.'

Cat sighed. In some ways – in her neatly swept lodge and gentle rebukes – Lark Sings reminded her of her own mother. Nevertheless, Cat was glad to have her hair washed. For the first time in her life, she wanted to look beautiful. It was a new feeling, a wish so strong it sent her heart skidding and thumping inside her chest.

* * *

Cat *was* beautiful. There was no mirror to prove it, but Cat felt it must be so. And Lark Sings, a gleam of pride in her black eyes, nodded to her and said it was true.

Cat walked along behind Lark Sings and her husband, Grey Lake. The beaded fringes of her dress swept the ground, and her freshly washed hair rippled past her shoulders. It had been Lark Sings' idea to leave it unbraided. 'Such a beautiful colour,' she'd said. 'Like a fawn without spots.' And then and there she had changed Cat's name to Fawn Loses Its Spots. It was clear to everyone – even Grey Lake, who pretended not to notice such things – that Girl-Boy was no longer appropriate.

The two young daughters of Lark Sings and Grey Lake, Rabbit Feeds Its Young and Gentle Rain, were along also. They walked in front of Cat, and she looked over their heads to the centre of the village, where cookfires glowed and smoke rose in tantalizing crescents. Curious eyes stared at her as they walked along, but Cat ignored them. Her own eyes, bright blue even in the firelight, were searching and scanning.

She saw his back first. Blue Quail was seated in the large, magic circle reserved for Blackfish, his friends, and his male relatives. There was not, and would not be, a single woman seated in the ring. Blue Quail, Cat saw, was between Tecumseh and Panther Walks, his back so lean and straight she would have known him anywhere.

Lark Sings, eager to present Cat to Blackfish, cut directly into the circle of men. Only a woman of Lark Sings' standing could do such a thing without fear of reproof, and Cat caught her breath when she realized she was to follow.

There were perhaps fifty men in the circle, and all of their eyes were now focused on her. Her chest tightened as if a bellows were suddenly opened inside it. She wanted suddenly to dart away from them. *I can't*, she told herself. *And I can't stare down at my toes like this, either – they might think I'm scared of them.* She raised her head at that thought.

Blackfish nodded at her approvingly, his deepset eyes the only part of his face that smiled. 'These are my sons,' he said, gesturing casually, the way a king might. 'Panther Walks and Hides the Sun and One Foot Bare and Black Shoulder; Loud Voice and Tecumseh, Blue Quail and Talks Little.'

Cat moved down the line, dipping her knees to honour each son in turn as Lark Sings had told her to do. But when she paused before Blue Quail, her knees locked. The movement of his arm rearranged his clothing, showing white skin beneath a buckskin vest. Cat's glance fell to his face. His eyes, set above deeply tanned cheekbones, were piercing blue, and the faint, telling shadow of a beard showed along his jaw. Cat froze. Blue Quail, despite his name and Indian ways, was white! He belonged to the same world she belonged to!

It seemed that she stood before him forever, waiting for his eyes to meet her own. They never did. When he finally raised his head, he looked at something behind her ear and beyond her shoulder. Cat moved on, her mind so full of thoughts that she scarcely noticed the warmer welcoming glance she received from the son called Talks Little – a son who, like Blue Quail, was also white.

The next morning Cat was full of questions for Lark Sings. 'You said Blue Quail was Blackfish's son,' she said.

Lark Sings looked up from the hominy she was mixing. 'He is,' she replied. 'Also Talks Little and the others.'

'But Blue Quail and Talks Little are white. How can they be his sons? How can they be Shawnee?'

'How can you be Shawnee,' Lark Sings replied, 'when you are also white?'

I'm not Shawnee! Cat wanted to shout, but she decided not to argue the point. Questioning her foster mother was an aggravating business. Although Lark Sings smiled and answered each of Cat's questions, it took a long time to get even the smallest scrap of information from her. 'Were Blue Quail and Talks Little captives too?' Cat persisted. 'Are they brothers?'

Lark Sings returned her attention to the kettle of steaming hominy. 'Of course they are brothers. They are Blackfish's sons.'

Cat sighed. 'They *can't* be Blackfish's sons – not the ones he had with his wife, anyway.'

Lark Sings laughed. 'Does giving birth make one a parent? Is not a parent one who feeds and cares for?' She paused and looked at Cat. 'Is that not so?'

'Yes,' Cat admitted.

'Yes,' Lark Sings said with satisfaction. 'So Blackfish is the father of Blue Quail and Talks Little, though they did not come from his wife's body.'

'They were captives?' Cat asked. 'Like me?'

'Perhaps,' Lark Sings replied with aggravating vagueness.

'And Tecumseh and Loud Voice and Black Shoulder and the others?'

'The father of Tecumseh and Loud Voice was killed in battle. Blackfish is their father now. The first father of One Foot Bare was also killed in battle.'

Cat began to wonder if any of Blackfish's children were his own. 'Is Panther Walks a real son?' she asked.

Lark Sings' eyes widened. 'And are the others phantoms? They are all real. They are all his sons.'

'I mean a son of his wife's body.'

'I think perhaps that is so,' Lark Sings replied, looking down. It was not proper, in her mind, to discuss such personal matters so openly.

'What about Black Shoulder?' Cat asked, driven on by sheer curiosity.

Lark Sings had had enough. 'It is not good for a Shawnee girl to ask so many questions,' she said, rising to her feet. She handed Cat a small hatchet. 'Will you gather some firewood for me? Take Rabbit and Gentle Rain – they will show you were the best wood is.'

Cat took the hatchet. Clearly, the conversation was at an end. She allowed herself to be led away by Rabbit and Gentle Rain, who were delighted to have her all to themselves. The two little girls seemed to regard Cat as some new and fantastic pet. They loved to stroke her tawny hair and look into her blue eyes. Now they jogged ahead of her on their plump little legs, eager to show her to the wood spot.

Summer had come without Cat's noticing it. The chill of spring was gone, and the sun beat down with steady warmth. Butterflies tumbled away in front of her, and insects hummed in the grass. As she worked to chop away the dry branches of dead trees, light sweat beaded her forehead.

'Hello.'

Cat's back went rigid, and she whirled around. *Hello*. It was the first word of English she'd heard in almost two months, and it made her vibrate like the string of a hunter's bow. She looked up to see Talks Little coming towards her. 'Hello,' she answered, slipping easily out of her Shawnee identity.

Talks Little was not tall like Blue Quail. His body was stocky and solid. His face was a careful mask. 'You speak English?' he asked cautiously. 'You remember it?'

Cat laughed, ''Course I remember. I've only been an Injun a little while.'

Warmth showed in Talks Little's grey-green eyes. The harsh mask dropped away, and he smiled at her. 'I saw you last night at the feast, and I been anxious to talk to you. It's been so long since I talked to anyone' – he fumbled, emotion cutting off his words – 'anyone white.'

Cat was alert. 'What about Blue Quail?' she asked. 'He's white.'

Talks Little shook his head. 'He's Shawnee. He doesn't even talk English.'

'I don't understand,' Cat said.

'Blue Quail and I are different. I've only been here a year. He's been here most of his life – since he was five, near as I can figure. Maybe his skin isn't Shawnee, but his heart is.'

Cat was silent as she absorbed this new information. The laughter of Lark Sings' children floated to her on the summer air. *Since he was their age*, she thought. *Blue Quail has been here since he was their age. Maybe Talks Little is right – maybe he is more Shawnee than white.* She stooped and began to gather the wood she had cut. Talks Little helped her. Their hands met over a branch, and Cat asked, 'Do you think about going home?'

'Every day,' Talks Little answered. 'Every day I tell myself that my real name is Richard Sloane and that, somewhere way back there, I got a home and folks. I've even got a sweetheart, if she hasn't given me up for dead.'

Cat rolled her eyes. 'A sweetheart. I got one of those too, I guess.'

Talks Little shot her a puzzled glance. 'You don't sound too anxious to see him again.'

'I'm not,' Cat said. She giggled, remembering Tom Alexander's adoring eyes. 'In fact, it could keep me out here forever.'

Talks Little took her seriously. 'Well, *I'm* not going to stay out here forever. I'm not going to turn Shawnee either, no matter how long I'm here.' Without warning, the brittle mask was back. Cat looked up and saw deep loneliness in Talks Little's eyes.

Cat felt sorry for Talks Little. By keeping himself apart from the Indians, he also kept himself apart from friendship. He'd earned the name Talks Little because he refused to speak to them, afraid that he would become too much one of them. But he had paid a terrible price for his aloofness. Cat looked at him intently. Was his way right, or was Blue Quail's? Was there a way to walk a path somewhere in between? 'I'm sure you'll get back home,' she said to comfort him. 'My pa is bound to be looking for me, and when he comes to get me you can come along with us.' She paused. 'What about Blue Quail? Do you think he'd come too?'

Talks Little shook his head. 'Blue Quail's a Shawnee. He'll never be anything else.'

They walked back toward the village. As they drew near, Cat realized that the air was filled with more noise than usual. Dogs were barking, and voices called back and forth. A strange sound, like a tinkling of small bells, filled the air. Cat saw a procession of ponies, each carrying a chief or warrior.

'What's happening?' Cat asked Talks Little.

'Whippoorwill Calls must be back. She's been away, visiting her uncle.'

'Who?' Cat questioned.

'Whippoorwill Calls,' Talks Little repeated. 'Blackfish's daughter.'

Cat grinned and shook her head in disbelief. 'Another child?'

Talks Little caught her meaning and almost smiled back at her. 'No,' he answered. 'Whippoorwill Calls really *is* his daughter.'

Cat was envious. 'Does she live in your lodge?'

'No. She lives with Tecumpease, Tecumseh's older sister.'

Again Cat shook her head. The living arrangements of the Shawnee were endlessly tangled.

The warriors parted, and Cat saw a girl seated on

a black and white pony. The pony wore a scarlet blanket, and the girl held her long neck at a graceful angle. Whenever she moved, tiny silver bells sewn on to her white elkskin dress danced, surrounding her with music.

Cat stood still, gripping the firewood to her chest. Whippoorwill Calls was beautiful – the most beautiful girl she had ever seen. When she smiled, her face rounded into an entrancing heart, and her long lashes half closed over her dark eyes, only to flash open again. Her satiny hair was divided into two braids, each bound with strips of scarlet cloth. Although she was not tall, she held her body as regally as the tallest queen. Cat did not need to be told twice – Whippoorwill Calls was indeed Blackfish's natural daughter.

Now Whippoorwill Calls was reining the pony to a halt. Cat saw her offer her hand to a brave and slide down into his arms. Then, as the pony was led off, Cat saw who the brave was – Blue Quail!

Like a drowning person floundering for a handhold, Cat clutched desperately at the wood in her arms. *Blue Quail!* Her proud, wonderful Blue Quail. Tamed, eager as a puppy for attention, he looked hopefully at Blackfish's daughter.

Cat stared at them, sick, at what she saw but unable to look away. The girl's silvery laughter mingled with the tinkling bells on her dress. Cat imagined secret meanings in her laugh, hidden messages in the glance of her dark eyes.

Realization washed over Cat like ice water. She had been prepared to fight the whole Shawnee nation for Blue Quail's heart – but could she fight Whippoorwill Calls as well?

As Cat stood wondering, another brave came up to greet Whippoorwill Calls. Cat saw the uneasiness in Blue Quail's eyes as Tecumseh approached. She saw the way Whippoorwill Calls gave the tall Shawnee her hand and the way she smiled at him – a smile as dazzling and full of promise as the smile she had given Blue Quail. Perhaps Cat thought, she had found the ally she needed.

Cat was unnoticed in the commotion the arrival caused. She was no longer an object of curiosity, as she had been last night at the banquet. The novelty of her fawn-coloured hair was eclipsed by the return of Whippoorwill Calls.

Cat trudged on with her bundle of sticks, her head full of thoughts, her heart full of sunlight and shadow, hope and misery.

Chapter 7

The image of Blue Quail with Whippoorwill Calls blazed across Cat's mind like sunburn. Just thinking of the way Blue Quail – *her* Blue Quail – had smiled at Blackfish's daughter filled her with choking misery.

All night long Cat tossed and turned with the memory, and she rose the next morning with the same thought on her mind. Whenever she closed her eyes she saw once again the dazzling loveliness of Whippoorwill Calls. How could anyone be so beautiful? she wondered. It simply was not fair.

Cat sighed unhappily. She had never given her own looks much thought before, but now they seemed unsatisfactory beyond words. She was too short, her hair was not at all exciting, and her eyes were china blue instead of inky black. As for her eyelashes, she didn't even know if she had any to speak of. And even if she did, she was certain that they didn't cast flirtatious little shadows across her cheeks the way the eyelashes of Whippoorwill Calls did.

Lark Sings had given Cat a basket of dried corn to grind into meal, showing her how to spread the kernels on a bowl-shaped slab and crush them with a flat stone. Thinking about Blue Quail and Whippoorwill Calls, Cat brought the grinding stone down with all her strength. It made a sound so loud that Lark Sings looked up from her own work. 'Is something wrong?' she asked kindly.

'No,' Cat said with a shake of her head. She continued her furious pounding. Corn dust flew from between the stones, making her sneeze. Soon Cat found herself wondering if Whippoorwill Calls ever sneezed, and if she did, how she went about it. Cat was sure the sneeze would be somehow lovely and entrancing.

Cat tried to imagine Whippoorwill Calls grinding corn, but she couldn't. No, she thought, surely Blackfish's blood daughter did not do such work herself. Cat's imagination leaped to the idea. She pictured Whippoorwill Calls whining and complaining as servants rushed to wait on her. It was the first consoling idea she'd had all morning long.

Cat smiled to herself. Why hadn't she thought of it before? Surely Whippoorwill Calls was bound to be spoiled and conceited beyond belief. All she had to do was draw Blue Quail's attention to that fact – then she would have her own chance with him.

Voices rang across the meadow, the same wide meadow where Cat had first seen Blue Quail dancing on the back of a pony. Now a large rectangle had been marked there, and two goal posts had been driven into the ground at either end.

Cat stood at the edge of the field, watching the game that swirled before her. Men and women raced across the field, fighting for possession of a stuffed deerskin ball. The object was to score by sending the ball through the opponents' goal. It was, Lark Sings whispered to Cat, the favourite game of all Shawnee.

Cat quickly understood why, for the game pitted the men against the women in a way that created tides of excitement. Legs and knees brushed against each other. Hands touched hands, and bodies fell together in tangled heaps. The women were allowed to use their hands or feet, but the men, taller and stronger, were allowed to move the ball with their feet only. Whenever a woman gained possession of the ball, a man would come racing towards her, shadowing her with his body and brushing against her in a way that sent shivers up Cat's spine.

A plump girl with dishevelled hair and bright black eyes caught the ball and began to jog toward the goal. 'Hurry!' Cat found herself crying. 'Run! Run!'

Beside her, Lark Sings chuckled. 'That's Many Rainbows,' she explained. 'She will not run – she wants a young man to catch her.'

'Which young man?' Cat asked.

Lark Sings laughed. '*Any* young man, I think.'

Now Loud Voice, the blood brother of Tecumseh, could be heard shouting above the others. His voice, deep as a grown man's, boomed across the meadow.

'Blue Quail!' he shouted. 'Come back into the game! We need you.'

Cat's head snapped up. Her eyes sorted through the maze of players. When she saw Blue Quail, a tingle of pleasure ran up her spine. Like the other young men, he wore only moccasins and a breech-clout. The afternoon sun glinted off his broad shoulders, and his muscular legs carried him across the field in long strides.

Before he collided with Many Rainbows, she turned and threw the ball to another young woman.

Cat heard a musical laugh and saw two slim arms rise like birds' wings. Whippoorwill Calls leaped gracefully into the air and came down with the ball, the fringes of her dress swaying as if she were dancing.

Blue Quail and Tecumseh both darted towards her, but she eluded them with a single sidestep, glancing over her shoulder and laughing as she raced toward the men's goal. Cat couldn't help admiring her movements. Men surrounded her, but Whippoorwill Calls always managed to dart away time after time, swift as a doe in the woods.

Finally, she neared the goal and sent the ball thunking between the posts. The crowd cheered, for Whippoorwill Calls was a great favourite with them.

There was a pause in the game while the scorekeeper tallied another point for the women's team. Whippoorwill Calls wiped her damp forehead with the back of her hand. Suddenly, her eyes fell on Cat, and she came dashing across the field.

'Fawn Loses Its Spots!' she cried in her musical voice. 'I have been wishing to meet you! Lark Sings, you are wicked to keep my new sister to yourself!' She grabbed Cat's hands and pulled her away from the sidelines. 'You will play with us, won't you? We are still three points behind the men, and,' she paused and lowered her voice to a diplomatic whisper, 'that Many Rainbows is *not* a help to us!'

Cat giggled, unable to resist the charm of Whippoorwill Calls. This was worse – much worse – than she had thought. Far from being spoiled and conceited, Whippoorwill Calls radiated warmth. She quickly introduced Cat to the other girls their age – to plump Many Rainbows and laughing Sun on the

Meadow, to shy Blue Apron and boldly curious Walks Soon. Cat barely had time to learn their names before the game began again.

Possession of the ball now went to the men. They controlled it with easy strides, kicking it to each other with their feet or bouncing it from their knees and elbows. There was something bold and teasing in the way they kept the ball away from the women, sending it flying just above their fingertips. Even Whippoorwill Calls, tall and lithe as a reed, could not jump high enough to catch it.

When a young man named Yellow Sky kicked the ball to Blue Quail, Cat discovered that being small was an advantage. Quick as a hummingbird, she darted under Blue Quail's elbow and flew away with the ball in her hands. A startled cry rose from the men's team, but the women yelped with delight. 'Over here, Fawn!' Sun on the Meadow cried. Cat passed her the ball, and she in turn passed the ball to Blue Apron, who returned it to Cat.

Clutching the ball to her chest, Cat looked up and found Loud Voice barring her way. His black eyes searched her face, and his broad lips curved in a challenging smile. Cat took a step forward, only to feel his body brush boldly against hers. She took another step, and again he pressed against her, close as her own shadow.

Cat's heart pumped rapidly. She tried to twist away from him, but her foot caught his and they fell together. Loud Voice laughed as she struggled beneath him, his breath warm against her neck and the weight of his body pinning her down. When they got to their feet, he was smiling at her. Cat still held the ball in her hands. Now she shot off across the field with it, racing towards the men's goal.

Loud Voice dashed after her, and Tecumseh and Blue Quail joined him in the chase. Cat heard their footsteps and glanced over her shoulder. Like all Shawnee, they ran with their toes pointed inward. It was a way of running that allowed them to cover long distances without tiring, but it also slowed them down.

Cat slowed her own pace, deliberately allowing them to draw near. She saw the insolent grins on their faces as they began to jostle her for the ball. Then she suddenly sprang forward and sprinted away with startling speed, running so fast that they couldn't possibly catch her.

Cheers filled the air as Cat threw the ball between the goal posts. She came to a breathless halt and turned, expecting to see Blue Quail's eyes on her. But he was already walking away, shaking his head as he said something to Tecumseh. Bitter disappointment filled Cat's heart. She did not even notice Loud Voice, who was looking at her with appraising eyes.

The game lasted until sunset, with the girls winning by two points. Loud Voice, who had scored last, came jogging towards them with the ball in his hands. Because they had won, Sun on the Meadow told Cat, the ball was theirs to keep until the next game.

Loud Voice handed the ball directly to Cat. 'Fawn Loses Its Spots is a swift runner,' he said, falling into step beside her. 'Her team owes her the victory.'

'Oh no,' Cat said quickly. 'We won together.'

But Whippoorwill Calls overheard them. 'Loud Voice is right,' she said. 'We could not have beaten the boys without you – so you must keep the ball until we play again.'

Loud Voice smiled at Cat. After he had left them, Whippoorwill Calls and Sun on the Meadow exchanged glances.

'I think that Loud Voice does not hold winning against you at all, Fawn,' Sun on the Meadow giggled.

Whippoorwill Calls looked at Cat with dancing eyes. 'Sun on the Meadow is right, I think Loud Voice likes you.'

Blue Apron looked at Cat with glistening eyes. 'Loud Voice is such a fine young man!' she cried passionately. 'His hunting bow is as large as Blackfish's! He let me hold it once, and I could not even pull the string!'

Walks Soon turned teasingly to Blue Apron. 'Ah, I think you are jealous, Blue Apron.'

Blue Apron spluttered and stammered. 'Not – not at all,' she said, coral showing in her coppery cheeks.

Walks Soon dissolved into a fit of giggles. 'Not at all?' she questioned. 'Why, then, were you trying Loud Voice's bow? Did you wish to learn to hunt?'

Their chattering voices hummed like insects in the air. No matter how fine Loud Voice was, Cat knew she would never care for him. He was not the young man she wanted. He was not the young man she had seen racing across the wide sweep of meadow on the back of a pony.

The only young man she wanted or would ever want was Blue Quail – Blue Quail, who had lost his world and his family just as she had. If he would only let her, she would give it all back to him, wrapped in the ribbons of her own heart.

Chapter 8

Whippoorwill Calls drew young men to her as naturally as tall trees drew lightning. It was easy to understand why. With her pretty gestures and quick laughter, Whippoorwill Calls was like a bouquet of flowers always in bloom. To stand near her was to stand in a golden circle of sunlight.

Cat felt lucky to stand even at the edge of that circle. The fact that Whippoorwill Calls drew her generously to the very centre made her ecstatic, not only because she liked Whippoorwill Calls but also because it gave her the opportunity to be near Blue Quail. For wherever Whippoorwill Calls was, Blue Quail was sure to be there as well.

Yet whenever Blue Quail appeared, almost always in the company of Tecumseh, he did not seem to see Cat. Her pale skin made her a ghost in his eyes, and if he noticed her at all it was only because Whippoorwill Calls insisted on it.

So Cat began to study Whippoorwill Calls the way her brothers studied the wings of butterflies and the insides of abandoned hornets' nests. If only she could learn to speak and act exactly as her friend did, she would have the same magic power over Blue Quail.

'It's no use,' Talks Little warned Cat when no one else was listening. 'It will never work.'

Cat bit her lip. Talks Little often sought her out, and his loneliness made her uncomfortable. Now she was uncomfortable for another reason; her feelings for Blue Quail were so private she didn't wish to share them. 'I don't know what you're talking about,' she replied stubbornly.

'Blue Quail, of course,' Talks Little answered. Colour rose in Cat's cheeks. Were her feelings really that obvious? Talks Little continued, 'There is nothing for me to do here but watch what goes on. I've seen the way you look at him. You want to win him away, back to the white world.'

'No, I don't!' Cat protested. But she wasn't a convincing liar. She knew that Talks Little didn't believe her, so she added, 'What if I do? What's wrong with that? Blue Quail isn't Shawnee – he's white.'

Talks Little's smile was bitter. 'Not in his heart. His heart is Shawnee. His heart belongs to the Shawnee.' He looked at Cat meaningfully, reminding her about Blue Quail's infatuation with the Shawnee chief's daughter.

'We'll see,' Cat said firmly. Maybe Talks Little was right about Blue Quail – but she would never believe him.

One day Cat and Whippoorwill Calls were cutting bark to weave into baskets. It was hot, tedious work, and they picked a spot near the river to catch the breeze. Before the bark could be peeled away in sheets, it first had to be pounded with the flat edge of a hatchet. Cat's arms ached. She laid her hatchet down and looked out across the river.

Sunlight fell in a golden haze, like a curtain, veiling the high cliff on the opposite bank. Fluffy tufts drifted from the cottonwoods, so light that they seemed to hang in the air forever. When Cat looked across at the opposite bank, she saw bright points of colour: flowering plum, tulip trees, dogwood so waxy white it seemed to glow. 'What a beautiful place,' she murmured.

Whippoorwill Calls, who believed a chief's daughter must set an example in all things, worked on. 'Is the place you come from this beautiful?' she asked.

The neat cabins of Brant's Orchard rose up before Cat's eyes. 'Yes, but different.'

'And your father,' Whippoorwill Calls said, timing her words with the rhythmic strokes of her hatchet, 'is he a chief?'

Cat laughed. 'Well, *he* thinks he is, anyway. We don't excatly have chiefs.' She squinted towards the high cliff of the opposite bank. 'Look,' she said. 'Tecumseh and Blue Quail. Loud Voice and the others are with them.'

Whippoorwill Calls glanced up. The young men saw them and began calling across the river. Whippoorwill Calls ignored them, but Cat's eyes remained on Blue Quail.

Trees leaned out from the high cliff, their outstretched branches quivering fifty feet above the river. As Cat watched, Loud Voice began to dance out on one of those limbs. 'What's he doing?' she asked Whippoorwill Calls.

Blackfish's daughter looked up and clicked her tongue against her teeth. 'Trying to impress *you*, I think. And, of course, himself.'

Cat saw Loud Voice smile as he swayed on the branch, his smiled challenging as he beckoned to Tecumseh and Blue Quail. Without hesitation, Blue

Quail began to climb out on to a second branch. Cat saw him glance toward the bank. 'I think now you are the one being impressed,' Cat told Whippoorwill Calls.

'It is a silly, dangerous game,' Whippoorwill Calls answered.

But Cat could not look away. As soon as Blue Quail stood even with him, Loud Voice advanced a few steps, daring Blue Quail to follow. Blue Quail danced out on the trembling branch. Hot sunlight beat on Cat's temples. The two young men inched farther and farther out on to the branches, and Cat held her breath, wondering who would be the first to back down.

Loud Voice took another step, and the branch strained under his weight. Cat heard a ripping sound as the branch tore away from the tree and plunged downwards. Cat saw Loud Voice's body hurtling with it, plummeting toward the water like a stone.

Cat gasped, and Whippoorwill Calls looked up. 'It's Loud Voice!' Cat cried. 'He's fallen!'

She watched the smooth surface of the river, but Loud Voice did not surface. Then a second splash ripped the water – without hesitation, Blue Quail had dived in to save Loud Voice.

A cold hand squeezed Cat's heart. After an eternity of waiting, she saw Blue Quail's head bobbing above the water. He had his arm around Loud Voice, and she could almost hear him gasping for breath. *Do something!* Cat prayed silently. *Please don't let him die!*

As if in answer to her prayer, a third body plummeted into the water. But it wasn't a god swooping down from the skies. It was Loud Voice's own birth brother. 'Tecumseh!' Cat gasped with relief.

A *thunk* that would ring in Cat's ears for years to come sounded behind her. She whirled around to see the hatchet turn over in the frightened hands of Blackfish's daughter. The sharp edge caught Whippoorwill Calls between the thumb and forefinger, biting deep into her hand and spraying red blood over her dress.

The eyes of Whippoorwill Calls were fixed on the river. 'Tecumseh cannot swim,' she said in alarm. She did not even feel the bite of the hatchet.

Cat grabbed a handful of broad green leaves and pressed them against the wound, trying to stop the bleeding. But the blood soaked through, rushing like a small red river. 'We have to go back,' Cat urged. 'I cannot fix this alone, my sister.' Cat, who'd seen accidents before, was afraid that Whippoorwill Calls would faint before she got her back to the village.

'In a minute,' Whippoorwill Calls gasped, for now she began to feel the stabbing pain in her hand. 'In just one minute.'

Whippoorwill Calls stared at the boys floundering in the water. Cat saw Blue Quail pull Loud Voice safely to the bank. But Whippoorwill Calls would not leave until she saw that Tecumseh, too, was safe on the opposite shore.

Cat slipped through the darkness, her way lit by the moonlight that fell across her path. The village slept around her, and only an occasional dog lifted its muzzle to sniff inquisitively.

She had come this way many times before – the

rhythms of her body did not stop simply because it was dark out. She remembered how her brothers used to make fun of her urgent dashes to the outhouse. The difference was that here there was no outhouse, only the endless woods.

Cat did not mind walking into the woods, for she had never been afraid of the dark. Besides, ever since she'd learned about the pony guard, she'd dreamed of meeting Blue Quail in the moonlight.

Blackfish's village was built in a huge circle. At night the ponies were brought in from the meadows and kept in corrals ringing the edge of that circle. The ponies were in constant danger of theft, for bold warriors from other villages counted a stolen pony a thing of much value. By stealing ponies, a young warrior acquired wealth and a reputation for bravery. By losing ponies, a village lost its means of survival.

To keep the ponies safe, four young men stood guard at night, one at each compass point of the circle. Cat went hopefully into the moonlight, always wishing that it was Blue Quail's night to stand guard, always wishing that good fortune would lead her past his guard post.

Tonight she saw his silhoutte in the darkness. Even from a distance she knew it was him. Only Tecumseh was taller, and Blue Quail had a way of carrying himself that was all his own. She saw his head cock at the rustle of her approaching steps. 'Who is it?' he asked.

'Me,' Cat said, stepping before him.

'Fawn Loses Its Spots?' he asked impassively.

'Yes.' It was the first chance she'd ever had to be alone with him – the next pony guard was a hundred yards away. She took her time looking up into his face. His nose, which seemed perfectly straight from a distance, had a little bump in the middle of it. She wanted to reach up and touch it. Instead she said, 'Fawn Loses Its Spots isn't my real name. My real name's Catherine Brant. Do you remember yours?'

She saw him stiffen. 'My name is Blue Quail,' he replied.

'I mean your white name.' He didn't answer. 'Don't you remember?' He looked away from her. She continued talking into the moonlight. 'I remember everything. I remember the cabin I lived in and my ma's cooking and the way my pa used to bellow just like a bull when my brothers fought in the house. See, we had this clock that came all the way from England with my pa's pa, and it was always in danger of getting kicked to pieces by my brothers.'

She watched his face as she spoke, hoping her words were candles to light up his memory. 'For a while, when Ike and James were at their roughest and tumblingest, Ma gave up altogether and put that clock in the cupboard. Now Deland and William are getting to the dangerous age, so I guess the clock's going to be back into the cupboard.

'But the clock's just in one corner of the room. In the other there's a big bed – Ma and Pa's – and it's got the most wonderful cover on it. A crazy quilt that's got a scrap of just about everything everybody ever wore. You remember quilts?' She fanned her fingers out, as if she were spreading the cloth before him. 'When I was little, my ma always let me play with the scraps before she sewed them. I'd sit on her lap and – '

She broke off, the words knocked out of her.

Blue Quail lunged past her, pushing her out of his way. Cat ran after him. 'You do remember, don't you?' she asked.

He kept his back to her. 'Go away now,' he said.

'But you *remember*,' Cat insisted. 'Don't you want to go back to your folks? I bet we could find them. My pa knows practically everybody, and when he comes for me we can ask him. Then you can come back with us. You can find your folks.'

Blue Quail turned. 'The Shawnee are my family,' he said.

'But your white folks – '

'Are dead,' Blue Quail finished for her. 'They were killed when I was taken.'

The shifting moonlight showed Cat the sadness buried deep in his eyes. 'Oh, Blue Quail,' she said, reaching towards him. 'I'm sorry. I didn't know – '

He danced away from her hand as if it were a weapon. 'So you see,' he said, his mouth settling into a firm line, 'I am a Shawnee.'

Cat planted her hands firmly on her hips. 'No,' she said. 'You *aren't* a Shawnee.' Blue Quail's eyes flew open in surprise. 'Even if your folks are dead, you still belong in their world. You belong in the world you were born in, just like me.'

Blue Quail, she saw, was listening to her. He considered her words. Then he said, 'I could not live in that world again. I am Shawnee.'

'You're as stubborn as Two Stars, that's what you are,' she said.

'Who?'

'Never mind,' she muttered in English, starting to walk away from him. 'I'll bring you around.'

His sharp ears picked up her voice. 'I doubt that,

Fawn Loses Its Spots. Blue Quail does not change his mind easily.'

Cat turned and grinned at him. 'But you've already started to. You've already decided that you understand English after all!'

Chapter 9

Whippoorwill Calls' hand was not healing well. In spite of the attention of Silver Spoons, who knew the art of medicine, her hand grew worse. An infection had started, and none of the healing poultices that Silver Spoons applied could stop it from spreading.

Whippoorwill Calls stopped going out of the lodge she shared with Tecumseh's sister Tecumpease and her husband. Blackfish was so grieved by his daughter's illness that his dark mood cast shadows over the entire village. Everyone missed the sunny laughter of Whippoorwill Calls, the young men most of all.

Cat and Lark Sings were preparing dinner one evening when Tecumpease appeared at the door of their lodge. 'Whippoorwill Calls wishes to see Fawn Loses Its Spots,' she said simply. Cat forgot about the dinner she was cooking and went.

Whippoorwill Calls lay on a bed of pine boughs. Although her face still had its lovely shape, her hair was dull and her eyes ringed with dark circles. 'Come in, my sister,' she said, gesturing with her left hand. Cat saw that her right arm was completely hidden.

Cat knelt down and rubbed her cheek against the cheek of Whippoorwill Calls, the Shawnee custom of greeting. A strong, unpleasant odour filled her nostrils. It made her angry to think that infection had invaded someone as generous and beautiful as Whippoorwill Calls.

'I have all sorts of news for you, my sister,' Cat began, forcing cheerfulness into her voice. 'Loud Voice wagered that he could shoot an arrow as far as Tecumseh and as straight as Blue Quail, and he nearly won! Sun on the Meadow's father has arranged a courtship meeting for her with a cousin from another village, but since Sun on the Meadow prefers Yellow Sky, no one expects much to happen, and – '

Whippoorwill Calls pressed her fingertips against Cat's lips, stopping the flow of conversation. 'Thank you, my sister. But that is not why I asked you to come.' Large tears welled in Whippoorwill Calls' eyes and slipped down her satiny cheeks. 'Silver Spoons says that I will die unless my arm is taken off!'

Cat stared at Whippoorwill Calls. The idea was unthinkable. 'But surely such pain would kill you, my sister.'

'Ai!' Whippoorwill Calls replied. 'It is not pain that I am afraid of. The gods will not let me feel that. But what will become of me without my arm? No one will want to marry me. And even if my father does find some poor, ugly man who is willing, how will I hold him in my arms? How will I take care of my babies? How will I be able to die and go to the gods with only one arm?'

She turned her face away, tears coursing down her cheeks. Cat drew in her breath. 'Let me see your hand,' she said.

'No,' Whippoorwill Calls said. 'It is too horrible.'

'Let me see. You are my sister, Whippoorwill

Calls. I do not think you are ugly. It is only the infection that is ugly.'

Cat nodded at Tecumpease, who came forward and undressed the injured arm of Blackfish's daughter. Cat bit her lip. It took every bit of concentration she had to keep from showing her revulsion. The wound had festered and begun to putrefy. Cat saw at once that Silver Spoons' diagnosis was correct: Whippoorwill Calls would die unless the arm was removed.

Unless, Cat thought, unless . . . She remembered a story her father told about saving the leg of a soldier by pressing a white-hot knife blade to the wound and burning away the infection. 'Whippoorwill Calls,' she said, 'there might be a way.'

'What?' Blackfish's daughter asked eagerly. 'Tell me.'

'It will hurt,' Cat warned.

Whippoorwill Calls arched her regal neck. 'I am not afraid,' she announced in such a way that Cat believed her at once.

'It is a way new to your people,' Cat added.

'I trust you, my sister.'

Cat nodded. Blackfish and Silver Spoons were summoned, and the heated-knife method was explained. Silver Spoons did not like the idea. 'She will harm Whippoorwill Calls with her strange ways,' he said. 'A white cannot give medicine to a Shawnee.'

Blackfish was thoughtful. 'Shawnee medicine has not worked for my daughter,' he said gently, careful not to blame Silver Spoons for Whippoorwill Calls' failure to recover. 'Perhaps the gods have sent Fawn

Loses Its Spots to us for this purpose, to heal my daughter.'

Silver Spoons, who needed to find the purpose in everything, liked this idea. 'Perhaps that is so,' he said.

Blackfish turned to his daughter. 'It is your arm and your life, my daughter. It is for you to decide.'

Whippoorwill Calls did not hesitate. 'I choose to let my sister heal me,' she said.

Cat did not want to do the healing herself, but Whippoorwill Calls insisted on it. 'Silver Spoons does not believe in this medicine,' Blackfish's daughter said. 'It is not his way. I trust you, my sister.'

So Cat cleaned the steel blade of a hatchet by dipping it in boiling water. Then she held the blade in the flames of the fire until it was white hot. Tecumpease and Lark Sings, with stronger stomachs than old Silver Spoons, held the arm of Whippoorwill Calls firm.

With one swift movement, Cat jammed the glowing hatchet against her friend's hand. A gurgle of pain hissed through Whippoorwill Calls' lips, and Cat saw her mouth go rigid as she bit down on the peeled elm branch they'd placed between her teeth. Beads of sweat showed on her forehead, and her eyes turned up in her head, showing only the whites.

The stench of searing flesh filled the air. Cat closed her mouth firmly to keep from gagging. 'There,' Cat said, stepping back at last. 'That ought to do it. Let's see if we can get it poulticed up before she comes to.' Sweat trickled from her armpits, and her stomach quivered as if she were going to be sick. She was relieved to feel the calming hand of Lark Sings on her shoulder.

'Tecumpease and I will do that,' she said.

Cat did not argue. She was content to stand, watching the two women smear herb salve on Whippoorwill Calls' mangled hand. Her knees shook as she tried to grasp the reality of what she'd done.

Whippoorwill Calls would not lose her arm, but her period of getting well was long. Silver Spoons devised a salve capable of softening scar tissue and, pleased with himself, spent hours massaging it into the injured hand on the chief's daughter. The old medicine man also decreed that until new skin had grown to protect the wound Whippoorwill Calls must remain inside the lodge.

Although Cat went to visit her often, the world of the village was not the same without Whippoorwill Calls. She did her work as usual, helping Lark Sings in the lodge or going with the other girls to work in the cornfields. But they, too, felt the absence of Blackfish's daughter. Even the plump and talkative Many Rainbows fell silent. It was as if the thread that bound them all together was gone and they had scattered like beads falling away from a string.

Early evening was especially lonely for Cat. In the free hours between work and the evening meal, she would wander far from the village, the mingling aromas of smoke and roasting meat filling her heart with homesickness. That was when she was most vulnerable – when lengthening shadows were capable of spinning webs of memory around her.

Her mother, her father, her brothers – where were they now? Were Ike and James and her father looking for her, or had they long since lost the trail and given up? Would she see them again, or would she, like Blue Quail, turn to forgetting simply to ease the ache of loneliness?

Cat brooded over her future. Where would she be in ten years? Would she have forgotten her white name and her place in the white world? The idea frightened her. Defiantly, she picked up a stick and scratched a bare spot on the earth, shoving leaves and underbrush aside. Then she wrote her name with the pointed end of the stick. Surely if she did that often enough – every day if need be – she would never forget.

She tossed the stick back into the woods. Now shadows coiled one upon the other, turning the woods black. It was as if the world ended there, rushing away to nothingness. With a shudder, Cat turned and walked quickly away. There were still light on the hills of the meadow and flowers to pick for Whippoorwill Calls. Cat was moving up the slopes when, far behind her at the other end of the meadow, she heard the hoofbeats of ponies.

Shawnee braves appeared like ghosts out of the settling dusk, their whoops filling the air. As she looked down, they galloped across the flat floor of the meadow.

It was the same scene she had witnessed the day of her arrival. Her pulse still throbbed with excitement because of it, and when Blue Quail burst into view, his hair streaming in the wind and his leg muscles flexing as he gripped the sides of the pony, a wild, sweet feeling welled inside her. She forgot the shadows of the forest and even the flowers she held in her hand. She forgot everything except that the world would always begin for her wherever Blue Quail was.

Chapter 10

Tecumseh rode in the lead, but Cat's eyes focused only on Blue Quail. He had mastered standing on the pony's back by now and was trying something new – clinging to the side of the pony so that his entire body was hidden from view.

Tecumseh circled back to look at him and soon was trying the same trick himself. But Tecumseh's long legs dragged on the ground, and Blue Quail shouted in a bold, teasing voice, 'You would make a fine target, my brother!'

Loud Voice, Black Shoulder, and Yellow Sky watched the two from the edge of the meadow, and Cat watched from the hilltop. Tecumseh tried the trick again, and again his long legs dragged on the ground. But Blue Quail was now dashing back and forth across the meadow, switching sides of the pony as easily as if he were climbing steps.

Suddenly, he dropped from the pony's side and lay on the grassy meadow floor. With a cry, Cat went spinning down the hill to him, dodging past Loud Voice and the others and almost being run down by Tecumseh's galloping pony. 'Blue Quail, are you all right?' she asked breathlessly.

As soon as he looked up, Cat realized she'd made a terrible mistake. His blue eyes blazed at her through narrowed lids. 'Why is Fawn Loses Its Spots spying on us?' he questioned.

Stung, Cat stepped back. 'I – I wasn't spying,' she said. 'I thought you were hurt and – '

Tecumseh galloped up to join them. 'It is a warrior's trick,' he explained, 'dropping from a pony as if dead, to fool the enemy.'

Cat didn't know what to say. 'Fawn Loses Its Spots should not be here,' Blue Quail insisted. 'Unless,' he added, 'she wishes to try riding herself.'

Cat's chin jerked. A voice boomed behind her as Loud Voice, overhearing the conversation, came to her rescue. 'Has Fawn Loses Its Spots decided to accept my offer?' Turning to Blue Quail, he continued, 'I offered to teach Fawn to ride,' he said.

No such offer had been made, of course, but Cat was grateful to Loud Voice for the face-saving lie. 'I hope Loud Voice is still willing,' she said. She looked directly at Blue Quail, her eyes turning steadily greyer and darker. 'I know the secrets of riding already. I wish to learn to stand on the back of a running pony!'

She had never enjoyed anything half so much as she enjoyed the look of shock that flared in Blue Quail's eyes. Loud Voice chuckled. 'That I cannot teach Fawn,' he said, 'for it is a trick I do not know myself.'

Blue Quail was looking at her. 'I will teach her,' he said, 'if she is still brave enough to try.'

Cat nodded her head to show that she was willing. Her heart began to thump in her chest, half in excitement and half in fear. 'Will Loud Voice allow me to use his pony?' she asked.

But Blue Quail had already slipped to the ground beside her. 'Fawn may ride my pony,' he said. Cat swung her leg up over the pony's back. 'You will get to your knees first, like this,' Blue Quail told her, acting out the motions on the ground. 'Then push yourself up slowly. Do not bend forward, or you will fall.'

She nodded and set off across the meadow at a trot, turning once and glancing back over her shoulder. They were all staring at her, and she could have sworn she saw the whisper of a smile playing at the corner of Blue Quail's mouth. She set her jaw in a determined line. Her father had taught her to ride as soon as she could walk, saddle horse as well as bareback. Standing up was another matter, but not an impossible one.

When she reached the far end of the meadow, she wheeled the horse around and began heading back. She brought her knees up as Blue Quail had told her, and began pushing herself up. But instead of keeping her back straight, she curved her shoulders forward. That ruined her balance and sent her plunging to the ground.

She fell with a thud, glimpsing the flying hooves of the pony as it galloped off. She got to her feet and set off after it. Grasping the reins, she pulled herself on to its back, determined to try again.

Cat fell three more times. Sweat beaded her forehead, and bruises began to show on her knees and elbows. She forgot all about the little band of spectators. She even forgot about Blue Quail. Her whole concentration was on the pony and the impossible task of standing on its back.

Angry at herself, she kicked the pony to a gallop and tried again. That was the secret, she realized. The jogging, uneven trot had been impossible, but the gallop was as smooth as a rocking chair. She flexed her legs and pushed up, keeping her back straight. Her heart thudded with wild joy. The meadow rushed by her, and wind kissed her ears. Small hairs on the back of her neck stood up with electric excitement. She was doing it – dancing on the pony's back exactly as Blue Quail had done! A cry broke from her throat, so wild and sharp it startled her.

She could not have felt closer to him if she'd crawled inside his skin. This was how he felt, this was his pony beneath her and his world swirling past her. And his voice, she realized at last, shouting approval to her.

Everyone was shouting as she galloped the length of the meadow – Tecumseh and Loud Voice and Yellow Sky. But Blue Quail's voice rose above the others, clear and thrilling beyond words, sinking into her heart like an arrow.

She slowed the horse, and Blue Quail rushed out to meet her. His blue eyes were no longer narrowed in anger. Now they sparkled with excitement and undisguised approval. 'Fawn Loses Its Spots is very brave,' he said '*And* very stubborn.'

Cat was still breathless from her ride. The earth slid and danced beneath her feet. 'I did it!' she cried. 'I did it!' It hardly seemed possible, so she looked to him for confirmation. 'I did, didn't I? It was not a dream?'

Blue Quail laughed. 'It was not your imagination. Fawn Loses Its Spots rides like a warrior!'

Beneath their tan, Cat's cheeks flushed red with pleasure. Happiness filled her to overflowing, and she didn't know what to say. Blue Quail's eyes on her made her even less sure of herself. 'I – I thank you for helping me and for letting me ride your pony,' she murmured.

'It is nothing,' Blue Quail said, his hand brushing hers as he took the reins from her. 'Fawn may ride again sometime, if she wishes.'

'Thank you,' Cat said, smiling with infinite happiness. A warrior's pony was a special thing, and to ride it even once was an honour. Blue Quail's offer to let her ride again seemed, to Cat, full of meaning. Perhaps he was, at last, starting to see beyond her pale hair and eyes.

Now he was looking at her from the corners of his eyes. 'Why *was* Fawn Loses Its Spots spying on us?' he questioned again teasingly.

Suddenly, Cat remembered the bouquet of flowers she had left on the hillside. 'Truly, I was not spying,' she told him. 'I was gathering flowers to take to Whippoorwill Calls.' She sighed and glanced at the slanting sun. 'Now it is late, and Lark Sings will need me to help with dinner.'

Blue Quail's face changed completely. A yearning, passionate look filled his eyes. 'Do not worry,' he said, not bothering to conceal the eagerness in his voice. 'I will be glad to take the flowers to Whippoorwill Calls for you!'

'But – but I – ' Cat stammered, the joy inside her going out like a fire doused with ice water.

'Truly, it is not a bother,' Blue Quail said. Already his thoughts were rushing away from her. The love-filled look in his eyes made Cat sick with envy. What had she done wrong? Why could he not look that way, just once, at her? 'The flowers are over there,' she said, pointing. Without hesitation, Blue

Quail dashed off, sweeping up the bouquet she'd left in the grass.

'Fawn Loses Its Spots has no need to be alone,' a voice said beside her, 'or to walk back to the village.' Cat looked up to see Loud Voice standing at her elbow. Despite his deep, booming voice, his words were as gently tempting as they were meant to be. 'Will you ride with me?' he asked.

Cat nodded, and Loud Voice lifted her on to his pony. His arms were strong and full of willing messages, but they were not the arms she wanted. The arms she wanted were flying away from her, full of flowers for the beautiful daughter of Blackfish.

Chapter 11

The hand of Whippoorwill Calls was almost healed. There would always be a mass of scar tissue between her thumb and forefinger – scar tissue that looked to Cat like slick bread dough when it was stretched and pulled. But thanks to the salve made by Silver Spoons, the tissue would be soft. Blackfish's daughter would be able to move her fingers as before.

Cat had saved Whippoorwill Calls' arm and perhaps even her life, and everyone in the village knew it. Eyes that had avoided her before now welcomed her. Even old people, wary of whites, nodded at her when she passed.

A young brave named Jumps High was heard one night playing his flute at Cat's door, the first sign of courtship. Afraid that Jumps High would turn out to be another Tom Alexander, Cat cried and begged Lark Sings and Grey Lake not to marry her off to the brave, who was almost ten years older than she was.

Lark Sings merely laughed. 'Do whites behave in such a lamentable way?' she asked. 'Shawnee girls marry who they wish. They are not expected to marry someone simply because he wishes it.'

Reassured, Cat breathed a deep sigh of relief, for how would she be able to explain an Indian husband – perhaps even an Indian baby – to her kin when they came for her?

Whippoorwill Calls assured her that what Lark Sings said was true. 'Shawnee choose,' she explained in her lovely voice. 'It removes a great burden from the parents.'

They were alone, with no one to hear them. 'Who will you choose, Whippoorwill Calls?' Cat asked boldly.

The eyes of her friend darkened, their fine glow clouding. 'It is not important,' she said.

'Not important?' Cat gasped. 'Of course it's important! Besides, I know who you'll choose.' Whippoorwill Calls looked at her with curious eyes. 'It's Tecumseh, isn't it?' Cat added. An expressionless mask settled over Whippoorwill Calls' face, but Cat saw sadness seeping beneath it.

'A chief's birth daughter does not choose,' she said.

'Why not?'

Whippoorwill Calls smiled a smile that was not a smile at all. 'My father may need to pay a debt to an ally,' she said. 'Or I may be needed to bind up a feud between our village and another.'

'But that won't happen, will it?' Cat asked anxiously. She remembered how Blackfish had sat entire nights with Whippoorwill Calls while her hand was festering. 'If your father knows how you feel about things, about Tecumseh, then he – '

Whippoorwill Calls cut her off. 'He does not know.' She glanced at Cat meaningfully. 'And he will not know. My wishes are not important.' Realizing that the conversation was over, Cat said nothing. Abruptly, Whippoorwill Calls changed the subject. 'I know a secret,' she said.

'What is that?'

'A ceremony. A celebration to honour someone.'

'Who?' Cat asked. In her mind, she was still mulling over the problem of Whippoorwill Calls and Tecumseh.

'It is to honour Fawn Loses Its Spots – to give her a new name honouring her skill with medicine.'

Cat's mouth opened. Her friend's words chased all other thoughts from her head.

Cat never discovered whose idea the name-changing ceremony was, but Blackfish had clearly given his consent. The whole village watched as Cat stood in a circle of firelight, her shoulders squared as Silver Spoons recounted the way in which she had saved the arm of Whippoorwill Calls.

When he had finished his recitation, Silver Spoons raised his arms and asked for the gods' permission to change the name of Fawn Loses Its Spots. Cat held her breath as she waited to hear her new name. Firelight glowed warm on her cheeks, and hot midsummer air pressed against her, bringing a fine sheen of perspiration to her forehead.

Healing Fawn.

The words sifted down on her like cool snowflakes. *Healing Fawn.* Her name. She felt an odd stirring of pride.

Drumbeats thumped to mark the importance of the event. The notes of a ceremonial flute fluttered in the air like butterflies. Cat stepped forward, her trailing fringes sweeping the ground behind her. She was wearing a dress of white elkskin, a dress almost exactly like the one owned by Whippoorwill Calls, with tiny silver bells stitched among the fringes.

'Will Healing Fawn accept this gift from her

father?' Blackfish asked, his deep eyes smiling at her. He slid a silver bracelet off his arm and handed it to her. Cat bowed her head to show that she was honoured.

Then Blackfish's other children came forward to give her gifts, Whippoorwill Calls first, presenting her with a magnificent sash starred with sky-blue beads. Excitement leaped in Cat's chest as the gifts were laid before her. Blue Quail advanced in the line, and she could not keep herself from thinking that his gift would be worth more to her than all the others put together.

The hands of her adopted brothers were full as they approached her, and Cat saw that Loud Voice carried a beautiful hide of tanned doeskin. But Blue Quail's hands were empty. Cat's excitement turned to fear. What if he meant to give her nothing at all?

Blue Quail paused before her with his empty hands. Cat raised her eyes to his, trying to read their message. Swiftly, Blue Quail reached up and removed the leather thong he wore around his neck. The silver coin that dangled from the thong flashed in the firelight.

Cat raised her cupped palm, and Blue Quail dropped the necklace into it. The coin was warm in her hand, full of heat from his body. Quickly, before the heat was lost, Cat slipped the thong around her own neck. The coin slid down between her breasts. She bowed her head to Blue Quail, her heart stammering with pleasure, her throat aching to tell him how happy she was to have his gift near her heart.

There was no dancing at the ceremony, for that would have spoiled the dignity of the occasion. But Cat's thoughts danced, and there was very little dignity in the way her eyes slid towards Blue Quail. Caught up in conversation with Tecumseh, Blue Quail scarcely noticed her. Not once did his eyes meet hers. Never did he give her the signal she longed for.

But Cat was not discouraged. Surely the coin had been a signal. It had been his way of saying that Whippoorwill Calls was not, after all, the only girl who caught his interest. Yes, surely that was what he meant to say. It was simply that he was shy of making his feelings known in public. When the ceremony ended and he walked away toward Blackfish's lodge, Cat stood looking after him.

'So, you have become one of them too,' a voice said in her ear.

Cat turned to see Talks Little. His face was sad and bitter. Her heart closed up, and she stepped away from him. 'What makes you say that?' she asked defensively.

'Look at you – Shawnee clothes, Shawnee name, Shawnee heart!'

Cat's chin went up. 'That isn't true!'

'Isn't it? Then I guess you'll be glad to know there's going to be a battle. I heard Tecumseh and Blue Quail talking about it. We're going to ride against a bunch of whites who ambushed some Shawnee down by Salt Creek. They say the whites are looking for captives. Maybe your father's with them.'

'My father wouldn't ambush anybody,' Cat said.

Talks Little shrugged. 'Maybe not. But they're looking for white captives – and they might just find us.'

Talks Little's smile was bitter. Cat felt sick. What

if her father and her brothers *were* with the whites? What if they came face to face with Blue Quail in battle? Two streams of feelings swirled through her, mixing together like hot and cold air in a stormy sky. She couldn't let her father and her brothers fight Blue Quail. Somehow, she would have to keep it from happening.

Chapter 12

The village rose early on the day the warriors were to leave. The men purified and cleansed themselves, sitting all morning in the meeting lodge while Silver Spoons chanted to the gods and poured water over heated stones, causing great clouds of steam to rise through the roof hole.

The women went about purposefully, keeping children quiet and preparing food for the warriors to take with them. Cat remembered how her own ma had cried and wailed when her pa went off to fight in the Revolution. But whatever crying or wailing the Shawnee women had in them they kept to themselves. Their smooth coppery faces were a study in silence. Even that plump chatterbox, Many Rainbows, behaved with dignity. Cat, however, did not have much time to observe their actions. She had plans of her own to see to.

After the purification ceremony was over, the mood of the village shifted. It became almost boisterous as warriors smeared themselves and each other with war paint. Each man had his own pattern – a pattern that made him look fearsome and awful beyond belief. Blackfish drew a line down his face, painting one half black and the other half ghost-white. Tecumseh covered his face, neck, and shoulders with red paint as bright as blood, then sat patiently while Panther Walks dabbed black spots over him. Blue Quail painted fierce black lines all over himself and drew a blue ring around one eye of his pony and a red ring around the other.

At noon the warriors mounted their ponies and rode away. Cat looked closely at the faces of the women, especially Lark Sings and Whippoorwill Calls. The round, girlish face of her foster mother was completely serene. Only a faint sheen in her eyes showed the tears hidden there. Whippoorwill Calls glanced once – only once – towards her father and Tecumseh. The men, lost now in the important business of war, did not look back at all.

The silence of the village without the men was terrible. Even the dogs, who usually barked and quarrelled among themselves, were quiet. In the afternoon, rain clouds drifted across the sky, shutting out the sun.

'Where are you going?' Lark Sings asked when Cat took her hunting pouch down from its wall peg.

'To see if I can get some rabbits,' Cat answered casually, 'or maybe some squirrels. With Grey Lake gone, we'll need meat.'

Lark Sings glanced toward the open doorway. 'It's raining,' she said in her gentle voice.

But Cat didn't answer her. Instead, she swung the pouch over her shoulder and slipped quietly out the door. Light rain struck her forehead and began to dampen the shoulders of her dress.

Cat skirted the edge of the village because she did not want to meet anyone. Her hunting pouch, packed full with a secret horde of food and clothing, dragged at her shoulder. There was a place where ponies grazed during the daytime, and Cat walked quickly towards it. She had already decided which pony to take – a mare that had been left behind because it was too small to carry a warrior's weight. But it would be just right for Cat.

An old man with streaming white hair sat watching the ponies, a blanket pulled high over his shoulders against the drizzle. 'I am taking the brown and white pony to hunt,' Cat said firmly, as if there could be no question about it. She tempted the pony to her with an ear of green corn, then slipped a harness over its ears.

The warriors had ridden out of the village with rituals and war paint, with wives and children lined up to see them off and Silver Spoons praying for their bravery. Cat rode out alone, rain soaking through her dress. The white-haired old Indian was her only witness, but he looked past her, his eyes fixed on the horizon where his own warrior memories danced. Even without anyone to see her off, Cat sat as straight as any warrior, her chin lifted against the drizzle.

She followed the well-worn trail out of the village until it reached the forking point. Then, instead of heading west, where the best squirrel forests were, she turned the little mare east. After a while, she picked up the trail the men had made earlier that day and began to follow it.

Cat kept well away from the men, knowing that if they found her following them she would be sent home. In two days of travel she came within sight of them only once, and that was by accident.

She had stopped to rest on top of a plateau that overlooked a stream. Suddenly, she became aware of voices below her and looked down to see Blackfish and his men crossing the stream. Cat lay without moving, the brown and white pony concealed in the brush behind her. She was well aware that the slightest sound or the least flicker of movement would draw their arrows.

As she watched, Blackfish slid down off his horse and waded into the stream. The day was hot, and insects hummed in the air. Cat's skin itched with envy as she watched one warrior after another wade into the cool stream. Soon they were splashing and diving like boys, their war paint running until bare skin showed through.

Only Panther Walks and Talks Little did not join in. Panther Walks stood on the bank like a sentry, bow poised in readiness. Talks Little merely remained on his horse, unnoticed by the others. Cat felt a sudden shift of anxiety. She had not realized until now how little she trusted Talks Little.

The men continued to splash and cavort below her, and Cat soon picked Blue Quail out of the throng. She watched as he dove into the water and came up laughing, his broad shoulders glistening, sheets of water rolling down the handsome curve of his spine. Cat shivered. She had been around boys all her life, but no one had ever affected her the way Blue Quail did. She knew that if he came face to face with her father or her brothers in battle, she would put her own body between them, no matter what the cost.

The nights on the trail were lonely and cold, but Cat dared not light a fire for fear of being noticed. Instead, she would curl beside the mare, chewing dried venison and listening to the shrieks and whoops of the owls.

On the afternoon of the fourth day, the docile mare became skittish. Its ears went back, and it danced sideways. Cat leaned forward to pat its neck and felt its muscles tense and quiver.

Cries rose against the silence. Cat's first thought was that all the owls in the world had come screamingly awake. Then she realized that the cries were human. Somewhere ahead of her, the men had collided with the party of whites. And the little mare, nostrils flaring, had known it first.

Burst of gunshot crackled in the air like lightning, splitting Cat's heart in two. Among the Shawnee, Blackfish alone owned a gun. The rest were armed only with tomahawks, bows, and arrows. Cat pressed her knees against the mare's sides, urging it ahead. The pony took a few steps forward, snorting and jerking its head so that Cat saw the rolling white of its eye. Then the mare halted, and no amount of effort would move it.

Frantic, Cat slid off the pony and looped the reins over a tree branch. Then she set off on foot, touching the knife in her sash to make sure it was there if she needed it.

She did not know what she expected to find. Her father had described fighting the British to her, telling her how the ranks of soldiers had moved forward in their scarlet coats, neat as the teeth of a comb. Had she expected something like that? she wondered later. Whatever she expected, it was nothing like what she saw.

Her heart was pounding from her wild run when she reached the battle site. She pushed through the underbrush until she found herself almost at the edge of a clearing, acrid gunsmoke burning her lungs.

Human beings struggled in a disordered, bloody tangle. Cat thought of the way chickens flapped around the yard after her father lopped their heads off with a hatchet. That's what the scene reminded her of, for it was full of the random idiocy of blood showering across the ground.

A bullet zinged past her, and Cat jumped back. She crouched down, hiding herself in the underbrush. Horses' hooves flew by her face, and a body thumped to the ground. She strained to see who it was – a white man, and no one she knew. Cat gasped and scrambled forward on her hands and knees. She began sighting the other white men in the group. Her pa and her brothers were not among them. The crushing weight in her chest eased a little, but she kept looking – for Blue Quail, for Blackfish, for Tecumseh.

She was watching when Panther Walks was killed, blood splashing down on to the fine moccasins his wife had made to bring him luck.

She saw Blackfish hit in the shoulder. The great chief's face did not change as, with a grunt, he switched the English rifle from his wounded arm to the good one, pulled his horse around, and rode again into the middle of the fight.

She watched Tecumseh kill one of the white men and seize his rifle before it fell to the ground.

She saw blood flowing everywhere, brighter red than any war paint could be.

And all the time she was looking for Blue Quail, skirting the brush that surrounded the clearing, so close to the fighting that any stray bullet could have killed her.

She saw him at last. He had lost his pony and was fighting on foot. Talks Little was beside him. Blue Quail kept his back turned to Talks Little as he fought. Clearly, he expected his adopted brother to protect him from behind.

But Cat realized that something was wrong. Talks Little wasn't fighting. Instead, he was shouting something in English, but his words were drowned out by the noise of the battle. Cat knew what he was saying. He was trying to make the white men understand that he, too, was white.

Suddenly, Talks Little abandoned Blue Quail and rushed forward. He grabbed the barrel of the gun that was pointed at him and turned it aside. Cat saw the look of surprise on the white man's face as Talks Little pushed his own face close to his and shouted again. Understanding, the white man pulled him behind him on to his horse. Talks Little, swept away from his home by a Shawnee war party and held captive for more than a year, had been heard at last.

Cat looked back at Blue Quail. He didn't realize that Talks Little had fled, leaving him vulnerable. Then, from the corner of her eye, Cat saw the long, slender barrel of a gun. It pointed like a black finger, circling and accusing as it searched for a target. Finally, it stopped, the muzzle aimed directly at Blue Quail's back.

Cat sprang forward with the instinct of an animal, mouth open to the burning air, hands clawing the barrier of brush that kept her from the heart of the clearing. The rifle flashed, and Blue Quail spun around, his body dancing lightly as a birchbark doll.

Cat felt the muscles of her throat contract as if she were screaming, but the sound of her voice was lost to her. She struggled forward and was almost clear of the brush – another step would set her free. A stray bullet *thunked* into the tree nearest her. Then there was another bullet and a hot, searing feeling at her temple. The day split open in front of her, and her hands lifted helplessly.

She felt herself falling, crashing back into the brush she had almost got free of. Brambles reached up with little fingers to pull her down with cruel, determined fingers. Her cheek was wet, and the wetness fell in front of her eyes like a curtain, but she managed to push herself another inch before she fell in the brush.

No one saw her hidden as she was at the edge of the clearing, not even the white man whose chance bullet had struck her. No one saw her small hand push forward beneath the undergrowth, fingers reaching towards Blue Quail like the shoots of a plant struggling towards the sun.

Chapter 13

The first thing Cat heard was the fluting call of a bird. Her eyes, sticky with dried blood, opened slowly. Bright sun streaked across the clearing, but she wasn't sure, at first, whether it was the sun of morning or evening.

She would have given all she owned for a drink of cold water. Her head throbbed. She reached to her forehead and traced with her fingers the deep gash made by the glancing bullet. Slowly, fighting the dizziness that flooded her vision, she pulled herself to her feet.

The world had gone away. The clearing was empty. The whites had vanished like smoke, and the Shawnee had melted back into the woods. The bodies of whites she'd seen fall were gone. So was the body of Panther Walks. The place where Blue Quail had fallen showed only a dark patch where blood had soaked the earth.

The battle was finished, and both the living and the dead had fled, leaving her alone. No, Cat remembered, not completely alone. There was still the little brown and white mare. She prayed that it had not been discovered or strayed from where she'd left it.

It seemed to take forever for Cat to work her way back through the brush, but there was the mare, blinking at her with round brown eyes. Cat rushed to it and rubbed her own aching forehead against the animal's sleek neck. She started to swing herself up on to its back, stopped, and tipped her head back. Sobs clawed at her throat and muscles, and tears boiled down her cheeks. She shuddered and coughed, gasping and gulping for air and twisting her fingers into the mare's mane. 'They killed Panther Walks,' she cried. 'They shot Blackfish and Blue Quail.' Her voice rose to a wail. 'Everyone's gone – gone!'

She cried until her face was swollen, round as a full moon. Then, exhausted, she simpled leaned against the pony. She hadn't dared to sob out the worst of it all – that she didn't even know if Blue Quail was alive or dead.

The patient mare shifted away from her, and Cat, using the last of her strength, hoisted herself up on to its back. She pulled the animal around in a circle, using the setting sun to point her way back to Blackfish's village. But the mare was strangely obstinate, choosing a course of its own. Cat gave the pony its head, and in a few minutes she was glad she had, for the mare brought her to the edge of a clear, sweet brook.

The mare bent its neck to drink, and Cat, too, plunged her face into the stream. The cool water soothed her aching throat. When she had drunk her fill, she dipped her hands into the stream, washing away the grime and blood.

The water left her feeling refreshed and strangely calm. She didn't realize until she took a wobbly step up the bank that loss of blood had left her lightheaded. She patted the mare's neck. 'It doesn't matter,' she told the pony. 'We'll get home all right.'

She'd said the same thing months ago, but then

home was someplace else. Now she spoke Shawnee to the pony, and when she said *home* she meant Blackfish's village.

Something rustled in the grass ahead, and Cat froze. She looked at the pony, who showed no trace of fear. As she watched, the grass rustled again. *I ought to look*, she thought. *Maybe it's a grouse nest with eggs, and I could use the food. Go on*, she told herself. *No use to be afraid now.*

But she was afraid – all that she had seen that afternoon had made her so – and when the bearded plumes of grass quivered again she almost lost heart. She forced herself forward, only to dance back in shock when she saw the body, half naked and covered with blood. It slithereed and struggled in the grass, clawing its way toward the stream. Beneath the dried blood she saw a pattern of black lines painted on tanned skin.

Cat's hand flew to her mouth. The body changed from a pathetic, slithering creature to everything she cared for in the world. 'Blue Quail?' she asked, swooping down beside him. His hand reached out, and his fingers grasped the fringes of her skirt. 'Blue Quail?' she asked again. 'It's me. Healing Fawn is here.' His eyes were glazed with pain, but Cat believed she saw recognition flicker in them. 'I'm here now,' she said softly, and Blue Quail collapsed against her knees.

The wound was high on his back, and she cleaned and dressed it as best she could, making a poultice of comfrey leaves to keep infection away. Getting back to Blackfish's village would be a more difficult matter, for the slight mare would go lame under Blue

Quail's weight. So Cat made a travois, uprooting two saplings for poles. She'd stowed an extra dress in her hunting pouch before she left, and now she slit it open and slung it between the poles.

It took the better part of the next morning for her to hoist Blue Quail on to the travois – the bullet, buried deep, made even the slightest movement painful. Cat saw his jaw clench and beads of sweat spring to his forehead as she struggled with him. But when at last he was resting between the poles, he thanked her.

It took them five days to reach Blackfish's village. Blue Quail drifted in and out of consciousness the whole time. His wound opened repeatedly, and he lost great amounts of blood. Because the bullet filled his chest with pain, he found chewing and swallowing difficult.

Cat grieved that the tough, rich venison in her hunting pouch was totally unsuitable for him. If only she could make him a broth or a corn pudding! Failing that, she would chew the dried meat herself until it was soft pulp, then put it into his mouth. That, she was relieved to see, Blue Quail was able to swallow.

His thirst was another matter, for loss of blood made him constantly dry. He could not move from the travois, and she had no gourd to use for a cup. Finally, she learned to dip her sash into the stream and squeeze the water from it into his mouth.

Cat saw no sign of Blackfish's warriors on the lonely trip home, and she was half afraid the village itself might have vanished in her absence. But on a hot afternoon she saw the first puffs of lodge smoke rising and heard the distant barking of dogs. When she passed the little gardens skirting the village, the women laid aside their hoes and stared at her as if she were a ghost. Whippoorwill Calls, who had been on her hands and knees pulling weeds, was the first to break the startled silence. 'My sister is home!' she cried, running towards Cat. She halted, seeing Blue Quail on the travois. His eyes were closed, and his face was pale.

'It's all right,' Cat whispered. 'He's alive.' Now that she was home, every bone in her body ached, and her head began to throb again. She swayed dizzily on her feet. 'We're home,' she said, putting her hand on the pony to steady herself. 'But if my sister would please ask Silver Spoons to come – '

Whippoorwill Calls was already running towards the lodge of the old medicine man.

Lark Sings was worried about the wound on Cat's head and wanted Cat to remain lying down.

'But I must talk to Blackfish,' Cat said. 'I feel better. I do, Lark Sings. Truly.' She was not lying. Silver Spoons had spread salve on the wound, and Lark Sings had bathed her and dressed her in fresh clothing. She had eaten two roast potatoes and part of the tender bird that Grey Lake had thoughtfully shot for her. Now it was evening, and she was anxious to talk to Blackfish. Reluctantly, Lark Sings said she would take Cat to her brother's lodge. Once they were there, Lark Sings tactfully withdrew and waited outside.

The Shawnee chief sat alone by the fire. For the first time, Cat noticed that there were deep lines crossing his forehead. His shoulders were rounded, curving like a great hunting bow. But when he heard her step, he looked up, and something akin to affection lit his eyes. 'I am glad you have come back, my daughter. I thought you, too, had gone.'

Cat was confused. 'My wound was not that serious, my father, to threaten my life,' she said.

Blackfish made a kingly gesture with his hand. 'That is not what I meant,' he said. 'Talks Little fled from us in battle, choosing the others even though they were not his people.' Sadness showed in Blackfish's face and in his voice. 'We are more his people than they. I did not think he would go against us. When we came back and Lark Sings told us you had gone, I thought perhaps you and Talks Little, together, had made plans. I thought you, too, had chosen the others.'

'No!' Cat was anxious to correct him. 'I followed you only because I feared my father and brothers might be there.' She kept her other motive – her concern for Blue Quail – to herself. Certainly Blackfish hid many secrets in his heart; she could keep a few herself. But his name was on her lips, and she asked, 'How is Blue Quail?'

'Silver Spoons says you truly deserve your name,' Blackfish answered. 'You did very well, Healing Fawn. But the bullet must come out.'

Cat winced. She had known it was so, but she hated to think of Silver Spoons probing that torn and ragged flap of flesh on Blue Quail's back. Deathly stillness filled the lodge. For the first time, Cat realized that something was wrong, dreadfully wrong. 'Where is everyone?' she asked.

Blackfish did not look at her but the fire as he spoke. 'My many sons are scattered,' he said. 'Panther Walks killed. Talks Little gone from us. Black Shoulder and One Foot Bare captured – '

Captured! Cat bit her lip. 'And Tecumseh and Loud Voice?' she asked. 'I have not seen them.'

'They mourn the death of Panther Walks,' Blackfish said.

'But they are all right?' Cat persisted.

'In body, yes. But in mind . . .' Blackfish sighed. 'They are changed by the death of Panther Walks.'

Cat wished to know more but did not ask. She had seen the body of Panther Walks high on its burial platform, but her probing questions were like the fingers of Silver Spoons as they searched for the bullet in Blue Quail's back. Instead, she drew a breath and said. 'It is very good that Tecumseh is not hurt, my father. It is a very good thing for the heart of Whippoorwill Calls.'

Blackfish looked into the fire for so long that Cat wasn't certain her words had registered. She believed that they had. When at last Blackfish looked up, his face was strong and dignified again. All of his sadness was hidden away. 'It is a good day, Healing Fawn,' he said. 'You have returned Blue Quail to me, and I am glad.'

'Then I would ask one thing,' Cat said.

'Ask.'

'That after the bullet is removed, I be allowed to care for Blue Quail.'

If Blackfish was surprised he did not show it. 'I will speak to Silver Spoons,' he said.

Cat was allowed to nurse Blue Quail, although Silver Spoons insisted on supervising things himself. It was decided that Blue Quail would remain in the medicine man's lodge, and, after a few negotiations,

Cat was allowed to move a few of her own belongings there. It was Lark Sings who had tried to bar the way, insisting that it was improper for a young girl to move into a lodge with two men. But a word from Blackfish changed her mind – that and Cat's own promise that she would return as soon as Blue Quail was better.

Blue Quail developed a slight fever after the bullet was removed, and Cat sat up all night long with him. A bowl of cool water was beside her, and from time to time she dipped cloth into the water and sponged Blue Quail's face and arms as he slept.

On just such a night, while Silver Spoons snored on his bed in the far corner of the lodge, Whippoorwill Calls appeared in the doorway. She came in and sat down beside Cat. 'Everyone is talking of your bravery,' she said, lowering her musical voice so that it would not disturb the sleeping men. 'First you saved my arm, then you saved Blue Quail's life.'

'Silver Spoons did much also,' Cat reminded her, in case the old man was awake and listening.

'Yes, of course,' Whippoorwill Calls answered quickly. She paused and lowered her eyes. 'Our father says you were looking for your white father and brothers in the battle. Is that true?'

'Yes.'

'Do you wish to return to them so badly, my sister?' Whippoorwill Calls asked. 'Are we not your family?'

Cat brushed a wisp of tawny hair from her eyes. 'You are my friends,' Cat said firmly. 'And now you will always be my sister. But I cannot forget my white family. Could you go away and forget Blackfish?'

The chief's daughter didn't reply. When Cat glanced at her, she found that Whippoorwill Calls was staring at her. 'I do not think it will be so easy for you to return as you think, Healing Fawn.'

'Why not?'

'Because your heart has begun to live here, with us. Because your heart loves Blue Quail.'

Cat started to protest but fell silent. Blue Quail fretted in his sleep, and she reached for the cloth again to wipe his forehead. 'I care for him because he belongs to my world,' she said at last.

Whippoorwill Calls wasn't fooled in the least. 'Did you feel the same about Talks Little because *he* belonged to your world?' she questioned. 'If so, why did you not follow him when he went away with the others?' Blackfish's daughter had inherited her father's impressive powers of reason. Her eyes, as they swept Cat's face, were wise. 'It is not the tie of a world that binds you to Blue Quail – it is the tie of a heart. I think you do love him. Healing Fawn, even if you will not say so.'

Long after Whippoorwill Calls left, her words lingered in Cat's mind. *Love*. She had never been in love before, and she wasn't even sure what love meant. Her brother George had fallen in love, and it had filled him with such silliness that the rest of the family had made merciless fun of him. Tom Alexander had fallen in love with her because she'd worn a pink dress instead of buckskins to George's wedding. Aunt Chess claimed to have been in love most of her life, but it had given her little wisdom that Cat could see.

Yet, as she sat there, the firelight rising and falling and dancing across Blue Quail's face. Cat knew that everything Whippoorwill Calls had said was true. She did love Blue Quail. The threads of her life were tangled up with his, and pulling herself free, if the moment came, would be no easy matter.

Chapter 14

Cat woke up suddenly. She hadn't meant to sleep at all – just to close her eyes for a moment. Now her body jerked in alarm, with the sure sense that something was wrong.

Blue Quail was trying to get up. Cat heard his rasping, laboured breath above the snores of Silver Spoons. She was beside him instantly. 'What's wrong?' she asked. 'Do you have pain?'

His handsome mouth winced. Then, in the low, red-gold light of the fire, she saw that he was smiling at her. His blue eyes danced with sudden life. 'No more pain than usual, Healing Fawn, but I was hungry. I didn't wish to wake you.'

Relief and happiness showed in her face. It was the first time he'd been hungry since being wounded, and she knew what a good sign it was. She touched his shoulder. 'I will get you something,' she said, raising her eyes to his. 'I will do it gladly, Blue Quail.'

He saw that her eyes, blue like his own, held pieces of flinty grey in them. 'Thank you,' he answered, lying back on his pallet.

She wanted to hum as she warmed food for him, but she didn't for fear her voice would rise, loud as a lark with happiness, and wake the medicine man in the other corner of the lodge. But her heart sang inside her. He hadn't wanted to wake her! Cat looked at that simple statement from all angles, the way a bride looks at her wedding dress. Perhaps he had begun to care for her after all. Perhaps her wild wishes and dreams were not impossible.

When the stew had bubbled hot over the fire, she decided to push things one step further. 'The food is ready,' she said in English.

He looked up, not even trying to hide the fact that he'd understood each word. But when he took the bowl from her, he thanked her in stubborn Shawnee. No matter, Cat thought to herself. She would try again.

The next day, she began making a pair of moccasins for him. Lark Sings had shown her how to cut the pieces from hide, and Whippoorwill Calls had given her small, brightly coloured beads to use for decorations.

Those days were the happiest of her life, Cat was often to think later. Silver Spoons had grown to trust her, and he would leave her alone with Blue Quail for hours at a time while he went off to search for herbs and roots. It was almost like being married. Blue Quail never questioned her being there, and he came to depend upon her presence. As his wound healed he slept less and less, and visitors began to come almost every day.

Tecumseh arrived with an odd, gloomy look on his face, but when Blue Quail asked him what was wrong he merely shrugged and turned the conversation to the cheerful subject of hunting.

Loud Voice came too. His eyes rested on Cat, and everything he said was meant to leave an impression on her. Cat pretended not to notice his attentions. Blue Quail, however, was irritated by them and said later, 'Loud Voice is nothing like Tecumseh, is he? Such a boaster!'

Cat ducked her head to keep him from seeing her smile. 'I think Loud Voice must be very brave, to have done so many things!' Her smile grew even broader when Blue Quail snorted in disgust.

Blackfish, too, came to visit. He and Blue Quail compared the healing of their wounds, showing off their ragged scars in a way Cat found childish and amusing. She said nothing but sat with the moccasins in her hands, squinting in the light as she sewed bead upon bead on them. She was intent upon her work, for she wished to finish them before she returned to her own lodge. And that day, she knew, would be soon.

But when Blackfish and Blue Quail began talking about Black Shoulder and One Foot Bare as if they were dead, she put her work down. Both young men had been captured in the battle, and Cat was alarmed that no effort had been made to retrieve them. 'I do not understand,' she said mildly, for she knew as well as anyone that a chief was not to be questioned. 'Why has no one gone to find them?'

'But they were taken by the whites,' Blackfish said. 'Surely their fingers and toes were cut off, then each of their other limbs, as whites do with prisoners. Then their bones were given to white women, who plant them in their gardens to make the soil brave.' Cat saw that Blackfish was perfectly serious. She couldn't help it – she began to laugh. 'What does my daughter find so amusing in the deaths of her brothers?' he asked sharply.

'Oh, my father,' Cat said at last. 'That is what the whites believe Indians will do to *them*.'

Blackfish puzzled over this piece of information. 'Why would they believe anything so outlandish?' he asked.

Cat looked at him. 'Why indeed? But I do believe, my father, that Black Shoulder and One Foot Bare may be alive.'

Blackfish's face lightened. 'Perhaps so,' he said.

The visitors brought news and laughter to the lodge, but the moments when she was alone with Blue Quail were what Cat treasured most. She would hum snatches of songs, filling in the English words and watching recognition flicker in his eyes. More than once she caught him straining to remember, but she quickly learned not to press the matter, for then he would turn away from her. If she said nothing, he would ask her to keep singing.

Blue Quail was young and strong, and his back healed quickly. On the day Cat was to leave Silver Spoons' lodge, she presented the moccasins to him. They were true warrior's moccasins, with long fringes that trailed at the heels to wipe away footprints. But Cat had chosen a pattern from the white world to decorate the toes. She had sewn beads there in a neat square, and each square covered the entire toe of one moccasin. It was an old quilt pattern called 'Log Cabin,' the most common of quilts and the simplest to make.

Blue Quail fingered the beaded toes for a long time, saying nothing. Cat longed to ask him if he remembered the pattern – surely he must have seen it before. She longed to ask him if he'd begun to remember how sweet the world he'd left behind really was. But she forced herself not to ask, as once she had forced herself to watch a caterpillar struggle from its cocoon without trying to help it.

There was going to be a celebration. Whippoorwill Calls and Sun on the Meadow came together to tell Cat the news. There had been some doubt that the corn dance would be held this year, for the battle had left a grim cloud over the village. But the death of Panther Walks fell farther and farther into the distance, and Cat's suggestion that Black Shoulder and One Foot Bare might still be alive had lifted Blackfish's spirits. In fact, the very next day, he had sent Grey Lake and two other warriors to search for them. Now he decided that the corn dance should be held as usual.

Cat was full of questions. What was the dance like? How was it done? What did one wear, and did men and women dance together, face to face, as whites did? But each of her questions went unanswered, for in trying to tell her everything Whippoorwill Calls and Sun on the Meadow managed to tell her nothing at all.

Lark Sings helped her dress on the night of the dance. Cat put on the white elkskin dress she'd worn at her name-changing ceremony and sat patiently while Lark Sings wove her golden brown hair into sweeping braids. She bound the end of each braid with blue strips of cloth that matched Cat's eyes.

Instead of wearing her ordinary moccasins, Cat wore a pair that reached to her knees. The moccasins had fringes running up the sides, and every third fringe had a small silver disc attached to the end. When Cat took a practice step, she saw that the fringes danced and jingled. 'You are very lovely,' Lark Sings told her.

But inside her fine clothes Cat was nervous. Why had she never learned, as other girls had, how to behave in such situations? The silvery laugh of Whippoorwill Calls, the way she looked at young men through her dark lashes – these things were mysteries to Cat. She had gone after Blue Quail in battle, had dragged him home and helped nurse him back to health, but now she felt helpless to command his attention. Perhaps, even after all that had passed between them, he would still choose Whippoorwill Calls as his dancing partner.

It was the sight of Whippoorwill Calls dancing that filled Cat with despair. No one could be lovelier than Blackfish's daughter. She moved over the uneven ground as if it were a polished floor, her deerskin dress showing the graceful curves of her body. Tecumseh was her partner. Whippoorwill Calls's shining beauty had even managed to dispel his glum mood, for he was smiling broadly at her as Blackfish looked on.

Cat stood uncertainly on the edge of the clearing beside Lark Sings and her two small daughters. She looked up and saw Loud Voice walking swiftly towards her. But just as he was about to reach her, Blue Quail appeared beside him. Taller and with longer legs, Blue Quail outdistanced Loud Voice by half a stride. 'I am glad to see Healing Fawn,' he said.

'I am glad to see Blue Quail,' she replied, lowering her eyes as she had seen Whippoorwill Calls do. She saw colourful squares staring up at her like eyes. Blue Quail was wearing the moccasins she had made for him!

Then she felt Lark Sings' elbow digging into her ribs. 'Put your hand out,' Lark Sings whispered in her ear, and she did.

Blue Quail took her hand and pulled her into the line of dancers. 'Do you know how to do this?' he asked.

Cat shook her head and watched his feet as he showed her the steps. The Shawnee dance was shuffling and dignified, but Cat could not help adding extra leaps and hops of her own. Blue Quail grinned as he held her hands in his own.

'Is this it?' she asked anxiously. 'Is this the right way?'

Blue Quail laughed. 'It is an interesting variation,' he said, but he did not let go of her hands.

At first Cat worried that he had only asked her to dance because Whippoorwill Calls was dancing with Tecumseh. But when Whippoorwill Calls, ever aware of her role as the chief's daughter, made herself available to other partners as well, Blue Quail seemed not to notice. Only once did he leave Cat, and that was to go off and drink refreshments with Tecumseh. When he saw Loud Voice dancing with her in his absence, he put his cup down and hurried to reclaim her.

It seemed to Cat that the drink passing from hand to hand had a dazzling effect on everyone. Blackfish grinned and danced with his sister, Lark Sings. Sun on the Meadow laughed loudly in a way that ordinarily would have brought rebuke. Old men acted as if they were twenty, and young men of twenty bragged as if they were old men.

'What is everyone drinking?' Cat asked Blue Quail.

'*Sofki*,' he said.

'What?'

'*Sofki*,' he repeated. 'A drink made of corn.' Now his blue eyes were sparkling down at her. 'I would bring you some, if you would try it.'

Cat nodded, and soon she was drinking the liquid from a gourd cup. It had an odd, sweet taste, a bit like the pickles her mother had made. But unlike her ma's pickles, it lit a warm fire in her stomach. The fire flamed gently, spreading to her fingertips and enlivening her feet. 'Delicious,' she said, handing the empty cup to Blue Quail.

The flutes and drums had only been background sounds, but now they took on a strange new urgency. Bold and giddy, she touched Blue Quail's arm. 'I would enjoy dancing again,' she said.

Blue Quail grinned, tipsy himself, and led her back into the leaping circle. The *sofki* drove what little she'd learned of the dance from her mind, and instead she did the dance steps she knew from the white world.

For a moment, Blue Quail just stared at her in amusement. But then he took her hands and, tentatively, tried to imitate her steps. Cat slowed down so that he could follow her. Soon the two of them were whirling together in a spirited dance that was all their own.

The Shawnee stopped to watch them. Cat heard Whippoorwill Calls' flutelike laughter and saw her friend pulling Tecumseh into the circle. Whippoorwill Calls picked up the steps easily, and Tecumseh had had enough *sofki* to go along with her. Soon other Shawnee took up the dance. The dignified steps of the corn dance were lost among the wild leaps of the new dance. At one point, Blue Quail circled her waist with his hands and lifted her in a sweeping arc, sending the fringes of her moccasins flying and jangling. Cat wondered what the folks at Brant's Orchard would say if they could see these fierce Shawnee struggling and laughing over a dance from the white world.

The *sofki* and the dancing left Cat hot and breathless. When she fanned her reddened face with her hand, Blue Quail suggested a better way of cooling off. There was a stream that branched away from the river and ran past the edge of the village. 'You could dip your feet in the water,' he told her. 'It is very refreshing.'

Cat nodded and felt a shiver of excitement as he took her hand and led her through the darkness. The moon was almost full, and its pearly light made shadows everywhere. Some of those shadows giggled when Cat and Blue Quail came near, and Cat could have sworn a shadow with a silvery laugh was seen leaning against a tall and very Tecumseh-like shadow. But at the stream there was no one near, and she and Blue Quail were alone.

They pulled off their moccasins and sat on the bank, letting the cool water rush over their legs. Cat felt Blue Quail's leg rub gently against hers. 'I never thanked you for the moccasins,' he said.

Cat felt his arm slide up over her shoulder. Exquisite happiness filled her, and she leaned against him. 'You are thanking me now,' she said.

His arm tightened around her. 'Healing Fawn, I – '

The proper Shawnee girl would have let him finish his sentence, Cat thought. But she was not a proper Shawnee girl and never would be. Her face turned up like a flower. Without stopped to think, she put her arms around him and kissed him. When she drew away, she saw the startled look in his eyes. 'Healing Fawn confuses me,' he said in embarrassment.

She remembered then that Shawnee did not kiss. 'I am sorry,' she said, her spirits dampened.

But Blue Quail lifted her chin with the tip of his finger so that he could see her eyes in the moonlight. 'What was that?'

'A kiss,' she answered in English.

'And how is it done?'

Her heart jumped. 'You wish me to tell you or to show you?' she asked. She could see his smile in the faint light.

'Show,' he said, his hand stroking her hair.

She tipped her head to him again and brushed his lips with her own. He was still at first. Then his lips opened to her, strong and forceful as a river, wrapping her in the two worlds she lived in and starting a thousand dreams in her heart.

Chapter 15

'It's a wonderful thing,' Cat said happily, pulling an ear of corn from the stalk and tossing it into the bag that swung from her shoulder. 'You really ought to try it.'

'With whom?' Whippoorwill Calls asked, reaching up to pick an ear that had eluded Cat.

'With Tecumseh, of course,' Cat snorted in reply. 'Kissing isn't worth anything unless you do it with someone special. I found *that* out last night.'

All around them, the cornfield rustled with movement. Women fanned among the plants, harvesting the ears that would feed them through the winter.

'I have no one special,' Whippoorwill Calls insisted. But her black eyes slid mischievously towards Cat, and she added, 'But I might try such a thing if I *did* have someone.'

Cat's eyes danced, mirroring the blue of the sky. 'Someone like the shadow I saw you with last night?'

Surprise showed on Whippoorwill Calls' face, but it quickly changed to a smile. 'Yes, with someone *exactly* like that shadow. How do you do it again?' Cat puckered her lips together and made a smacking sound. Whippoorwill Calls looked dubious. 'And that makes one feel joyful?'

'*Very* joyful,' Cat assured her.

Whippoorwill Calls still was not convinced. 'Did you invent this thing yourself? Perhaps it is just that odd things make you joyful.'

Cat giggled. 'Oh no,' she said. '*Everybody* where I come from kisses.'

A frown fell like a shadow across Whippoorwill Calls' face. 'It is a thing of the white world?' she asked.

'Yes.'

Blackfish's daughter shook her head. 'Then I do not think even Tecumseh's shadow would try it,' she said sadly.

Cat looked at her for a long moment. 'Whippoorwill Calls, what's wrong with Tecumseh? Ever since the battle – '

Whippoorwill Calls nodded. 'The death of Panther Walks is a little death in his own heart, I think. And more than that, the running away of Talks Little . . .'

Cat had long ago forgiven Talks Little in her own mind and heart. 'Does Tecumseh blame Talks Little for wanting to go back to his own people?' Cat asked.

'No,' Whippoorwill Calls said. 'He does not blame him. But it has made him think. It has made him decide that the white world and the Indian world can never be one. It has made him decide that Shawnee people should have nothing to do with white people or white ways. Even captives.'

Cat's chin jerked up. 'But *I'm* white,' she said. 'So is Blue Quail! Does Tecumseh want nothing to do with *us*?'

Whippoorwill Calls did not answer the question. Instead, she put out her hand. 'You will always be my sister,' she said, 'no matter what world you are in, isn't that so?'

'Yes,' Cat answered, glad to know that Whippoorwill Calls did not share Tecumseh's harsh point of view.

'Do not be angry with Tecumseh,' Whippoorwill Calls said when Cat fell silent.

But Cat's mind was no longer with Tecumseh. 'I'm not angry with him,' she said. 'But I *do* hate to think of you never kissing.' Her brow wrinkled in thought. 'Is it completely necessary to tell him it's a white custom?'

Whippoorwill Calls laughed. 'But what if he asks?'

Cat grinned at her. 'If you do it the right way, he won't ask.'

That night a flute was heard outside the lodge of Lark Sings. Cat felt a happy flush spread across her cheeks. All day long, a question had waited underneath her happiness. Did Blue Quail feel the same way she did – *exactly* the same way she did? Or had it only been *sofki* and moonlight that made him kiss her? Now the piping sounds of the flute answered her question.

At the sound of the flute, Lark Sings' little girls ran to the door and peeped out. 'It's Loud Voice!' Rabbit Feeds Its Young cried.

Loud Voice! Cat's eyes flew open in surprise. Lark Sings snatched Rabbit away from the door and pulled her down on to her lap. 'Come here, little chatterbox,' she scolded. 'He certainly has not come to court *you*!'

Cat put aside the pouch she was stitching – a game pouch she meant to give Blue Quail. She looked at Lark Sings in confusion. 'I do not understand,' she said. 'Loud Voice?'

Lark Sings smiled wisely. 'Sometimes the interest of one young man makes the interest of another grow stronger, is that not so?'

Cat's light brown eyebrows grew together. She planted her chin in her palm and said, 'I don't know. I never had much experience with young men, except my brothers.'

Lark Sings giggled like a girl. 'One does not need experience to know certain things.'

The flute music throbbed in the air, impossible to ignore. 'What do I do?' Cat asked.

'Do you wish to encourage Loud Voice? He is a most promising young man.'

Cat shook her head. Loud Voice *was* a promising young man. But he was not Blue Quail. 'No,' she said.

'Then it is best to do nothing,' Lark Sings advised.

'Nothing?' Cat asked. 'You mean I should just let him stand out there? But that seems cruel!'

Lark Sings shrugged. 'That is the way courting is done. When I was your age, three braves courted me at once. I liked Grey Lake all along, but I waited two weeks before encouraging him, and then I did it only because the courting noise gave my father headaches!'

Cat giggled. Still, she didn't like to think of Loud Voice sitting outside the lodge for two weeks. She rose to her feet, prepared to go to the door and send him away. But as she did, a second flute sounded, its notes leaping up like bright, vibrant flames. Cat stopped, the firelight heating her face.

Lark Sings smiled. 'It is as I said,' she told Cat.

'The interest of one young man sometimes makes the interest of another grow stronger.' She bent her head and whispered to Rabbit Feeds Its Young. 'Perhaps my little chatterbox could creep quietly to the door and see who it is *without* shouting his name for the whole village to hear!'

Rabbit crept to the door with exaggerated stealth, determined to prove worthy of her important task. She came back with a smile on her face. 'It's Blue Quail!' she whispered.

Lark Sings looked at Cat expectantly. 'Does Healing Fawn wish to encourage him?'

Cat listened to the music, her happiness larger than the starry sky that peeked through the roof hole. Yes, she wished to encourage him, but she did not go bouncing to the door as her feet longed to do. Blue Quail had ignored her for weeks while she had panted for a single glance from him. And now, tonight, he had not even thought to come courting until Loud Voice led the way! She looked at Lark Sings. 'I do not see any particular hurry,' she smiled.

Lark Sings laughed. 'For one with no experience, Healing Fawn is not altogether unwise,' she said.

The next day, Whippoorwill Calls told Cat she had done exactly the right thing. 'Only girls who fear they cannot get husbands appear at the door the first night,' she said. 'Or girls who are so eager that the sight of a boy drives the brains from their heads. Many Rainbows, I am sure, will go racing away with the first young man who speaks for her.' She stepped back and looked at Cat's lovely honey-coloured braids and glinting blue eyes. 'My sister is very pretty,' she said in appraisal. 'You can afford to choose.'

'Oh, I have already chosen,' Cat said. 'It is just that I wish to make the chosen one suffer a little while.' It was odd, she thought. She wanted to spare Loud Voice pain and disappointment, though she did not love him. But Blue Quail, whom she loved with her whole heart, she wished to gently torture.

Whippoorwill Calls understood completely. 'Then you did exactly as you should have done,' she said. Cat thought it was a pity that Whippoorwill Calls' standing as Blackfish's blood daughter kept her from playing such courting games herself. What fights and heartbreaks she could cause if she wished to!

That night the two flutes returned to play for Cat, and the next night as well. On the fourth night, Blue Quail laid aside his instrument and began to sing, determined to drown out Loud Voice.

Cat listened in horror. Blue Quail had no voice for singing. In fact, he sounded much like a wounded goose. When two dogs joined in, lifting their muzzles and yowling in unison, Cat had to press her hand against her mouth to stifle her laughter.

Blue Quail surely knew how terrible his voice was, but he sang on bravely. After a while, Lark Sings looked up from the winter moccasins she was stitching. 'Even a determined suitor will lose heart eventually,' she said mildly. 'Especially if he becomes a laughingstock.'

Cat looked across the fire at her. 'Perhaps it is time to choose?'

'Perhaps it is,' Lark Sings said.

Cat reached into the neck of her dress and pulled

the coin Blue Quail had given her to the outside. Then she ducked out the low door of the lodge.

Loud Voice stood to the left and Blue Quail to the right. The moon had begun to wane, and it was difficult to make out the expressions of their faces. Cat had discussed this moment with Whippoorwill Calls, and she knew exactly what to do. Looking down, she lifted her right hand. The flute music stopped abruptly, and she heard Loud Voice's footsteps fading away into the night. Then she felt Blue Quail take the hand she offered him, and she heard his voice in her ear saying, 'I am glad, Healing Fawn.'

She smiled down at her moccasins. 'It is just that I have pity for the ears of this village,' she said, 'and for the owner of such a poor voice. Surely you could win no other girl with such screaming!'

He pulled her to him. 'I want no other girl!' he said. 'No other fills my heart the way Healing Fawn does!'

She could resist him no longer, not even for his own good. Her arms slid around his neck, and she stood on her tiptoes. He was so tall that he still had to bend slightly to meet her lips. They kissed, and Cat drew away from him breathlessly. 'You did not forget how to do this,' she murmured.

Blue Quail chuckled, his blue eyes glistening in the pale light. 'I did not forget.'

Cat looked at him sharply. 'You haven't been practising with anyone else, have you?'

'Of course not,' he said. 'But I have been thinking much of Healing Fawn.' He caught her face between his hands and kissed her again. His lips wandered boldly from her lips to her cheek, from her cheek to the pink shell of her ear, and finally to the sensitive skin of her throat.

Cat's knees quivered. The world seemed to pitch beneath her, and she felt a wild, breathless excitement spreading through her. It was like standing on the back of a galloping pony, only safer, with strong, welcoming arms to catch her. 'Oh,' she gasped, pressing herself so close to him that she could feel their two hearts fluttering together.

Blue Quail pulled himself gently away. 'Why don't we walk a while?' he said. 'Standing too close to you isn't good for me.'

Cat was glad that the darkness hid her blush. She knew enough of boys – of men – to know what he meant. So she slipped her hand into his and let him lead her away from the clustered lodges of the village.

Sifting moonlight spread deliciously around them, wrapping them in a world of their own. A gentle breeze, cool with the taste of autumn, rustled past them. Cat shivered, and Blue Quail pressed her close to him. His eyes caught the gleam of silver at her neck, and he touched the coin he'd given her, first with his finger, then with his lips. 'I will get Healing Fawn a necklace of gold instead,' he said. 'A necklace made entirely of gold coins!'

Cat clutched the little silver coin protectively. 'I don't want a different necklace!' she said in alarm, afraid he might snatch the thong from her neck. 'This was Blue Quail's first present to me, and I will never take it off!'

Her jutting, determined chin bumped against his shoulder. 'If that is what you wish,' he said, 'Perhaps, instead, you will let me offer gifts to Blackfish, to Lark Sings and Grey Lake.'

Dazzled, Cat did not understand his meaning. 'Why?' she asked.

He turned her to him and looked down at her. His handsome face was serious. 'Does Healing Fawn not wish to be my wife?'

Her mouth dropped open. 'I – I'm – yes, but I'm only sixteen!'

Blue Quail smiled at her. 'That's old enough for a Shawnee.'

Her eyes shifted from blue to grey. 'I am *not* a Shawnee,' she said stubbornly. 'Neither are you.'

A tense silence passed between them. After a moment, Blue Quail said, 'I still wish you to be my wife. Will you?'

The knitting needle that had been jabbing Cat's ribs began to go away, but she would not back down completely. 'Yes,' she said in English.

'Good,' he replied in Shawnee, and they kissed so fiercely that their front teeth scraped together. 'I will talk to Blackfish. And to Grey Lake, too, when he returns.'

Cat was restless in his arms. She remembered how Blackfish had had to give up his silver armbands to buy her from Two Stars. 'Will I cost you money?' she asked.

Blue Quail laughed and kissed the top of her head. 'Ponies, not money,' he said.

She looked up at him in alarm. 'But we'll need the ponies.'

'What for?'

Cat bit her lip. 'Because of what I said before – we're *white* people. We belong in the white world, not in this one. Isn't that what Tecumseh has decided?' She saw him wince at that and changed her tactic. 'I can't live my life here, Blue Quail,' she went on. 'Even if my folks have given up looking for me, I've got to look for *them*. You've got to take me back, don't you see?'

Cat's voice had risen to a plaintive wail. Blue Quail stepped back away from her. 'But I *don't* belong there,' he said. 'Not anymore. Would I have any place there? Would I not die if I lived in a town?'

Cat clutched his hands. 'But Brant's Orchard isn't a *town*!' she cried. 'It's smaller than here, and we could – oh, Blue Quail, we could move farther west. We could build just across the river. It's the wildest, sweetest place on earth. It would be our world, just ours – *ours*!'

He turned away from her, his chest rising and falling in the moonlight. That was when she saw, for the first time, that he was afraid – afraid to venture into her world. A panicky fear caught at her throat. She felt him slipping away from her, shutting his heart to her. She put a hand on his shoulder, but he stepped away, and her hand fell through the silvery webs of moonlight.

Chapter 16

The next night, there was no singing and no flute music outside the lodge. Lark Sings looked at Cat curiously, but Cat kept her eyes on the small moccasin she was making for Rabbit Feeds Its Young.

She had not seen Blue Quail all day long, and not seeing him had left an empty place inside her. Cat would not show it, but she was waiting. She bit her lip anxiously as she worked the bone needle through the plaint moccasin leather.

She was not even sure how the quarrel had started. One moment they'd been kissing, and the next moment they'd stood apart, he in one world and she in another. Cat remembered how the moonlight had fallen between them, cool and luminous as ice.

But surely he would come back she told herself. And when he did, she would toss aside the moccasin and go running out to him. All that mattered was for them to be together. But Blue Quail didn't come, and Cat sat through the long evening. Each stab of her bone needle seemed to slide through the moccasin leather and into her own heart.

The following day, Cat asked Whippoorwill Calls for advice. To her surprise, the chief's daughter was remarkably lighthearted. 'Everything will turn out well, Healing Fawn,' she said, as calmly as if she were discussing a turn in the weather. 'Do not worry, Such things usually do work themselves out, no matter what one thinks.'

'But it's been two days now,' Cat wailed. 'I haven't seen him anywhere.'

'When he wants you to see him, you will,' Whippoorwill Calls replied with an unruffled smile.

Cat frowned, her light brown eyebrows drawing together. 'That's what worries me,' she said. 'What if he *never* wants to see me?'

Whippoorwill Calls refused to share her friend's anxiety. 'I am sure he'll want to see you, Healing Fawn.'

'How can you be sure?' Cat demanded. Whippoorwill Calls' casual attitude was beginning to annoy her.

Blackfish's daughter smiled and shrugged her shoulders. 'Well, that kissing thing alone may bring him back.'

Cat saw a delicious smile blossom on her friend's face. So that was it! 'You tried it, didn't you? You tried it with – '

Whippoorwill Calls jostled her elbow before she could continue. 'A shadow,' she said, in case anyone was listening.

'And you liked it?'

Whippoorwill Calls looked at her through a fringe of sooty lashes. 'It was most pleasing.'

'And the shadow?'

Whippoorwill Calls began to giggle. 'I do not recall that he complained.'

They were walking along a path, balancing on their hips the baskets of wild autumn grapes they'd picked. Whippoorwill Calls slowed her pace and clutched Cat's hand. 'There is something more, too,' she said, lowering her voice to whisper.

'What?' Cat asked eagerly.

'Tecum – um, the, ah, *shadow* wishes to speak to my father.'

Cat wanted to jump up and down right there, no matter how much attention it might attract. But she restrained herself. 'Oh, I am so happy for you, Whippoorwill Calls!'

That night, Tecumseh began to court the chief's daughter in earnest, leaving presents at her door and playing music for her. The next day, the whole village buzzed with the news. But the cheerful speculations and the sounds of drifting flute music filled Cat with memories and loneliness. Blue Quail had avoided her for four days How many more days did he mean to stay away? Or did he mean never to return at all?

She needed to be by herself for a while, Cat decided. She needed to be alone, far from the chatter and gaiety of Whippoorwill Calls' courtship. Grey Lake's absence provided the perfect excuse. She packed her hunting pouch, took her slingshot, and told Lark Sings she was going into the woods to look for meat. If she did not return for a few days, no one was to worry.

Cat knew that Lark Sings saw through this excuse, but it didn't matter. All that mattered was that she get away, to someplace where Blue Quail's nearness did not torment her. Her heart was exhausted with waiting for him.

She did not take a pony but went on foot, discovering a world singed with the fiery colours of autumn. It had been a dry summer, with less rain than usual. The cool weather had come swiftly, crisping the dry leaves and filling them with vivid colour. She reached the top of a stony gorge and gasped in wonder. The orange and yellow trees stood out like brightly feathered birds. Below her, water tumbled through a cataract into the narrow plume of a silvery stream below. Deer came to drink there, their delicate hooves tapping the rocks, their antlers spreading magnificently.

Tears rolled down Cat's cheeks. It was all so lovely! Lovelier than Blackfish's village and lovelier – though she hated to admit it – than Brant's Orchard. If only Blue Quail could see it, she knew he would agree with her. This was the world the two of them belonged in – a world that was neither white nor Indian.

Cat sighed and felt her tears grow cold on her face. Summer was gone, and winter lay ahead. She had been captured more than half a year ago, and no one had come for her. She tried to look ahead, but her future was a puzzling blank. It was like looking for solid ground beyond the edge of the gorge – there was simply nothing there to see.

The sun set early, and even Cat's small fire could not keep her awake. She fell asleep beneath a ledge at the top of the gorge, beauty drifting all around her but loneliness lodged in her heart as stubbornly as ever.

Cat had good luck finding game, and on the third day she was preparing to go back. It began as a cool, dry day filled with dazzling light. But at midmorning the sky turned deep blue. Looking up at it was like looking into the vault of heaven, Cat thought. It went on forever, shades of blue upon blue, clear as the glass marble her brother James had once owned.

By noon, towering clouds appeared, tall and grey as chimney smoke, blocking out the sun. *Just my luck,* Cat thought. *It hasn't stormed for weeks, and now I'm going to get caught in one.* There was no sense hurrying her steps, for even if she ran she couldn't get back to the village in time. Instead, she began looking around for a cave or a wide ledge. *Never wait out a storm under a tree*, her pa had always told her. *A tree's the first place lightning hits*. So when she saw a shallow cave, she ducked into it. Looking out, she could see the patchwork hills rolling away into the distance.

Lightning flashed in the air above her, splitting the heart of a monstrous cloud. Thunder shook the earth beneath her. Cat waited for the sound of rain, but only a few fat drops spattered in front of the cave. She hugged her knees against her chest and shivered, for the air had turned cold, and a fierce, chilling wind had sprung up.

More bolts of lightning came, each with its terrific boom of thunder. Cat laid her cheek against her knees, anxious for the storm to be over. Suddenly, she found herself hungry for the hum of human voices – anxious for the soothing chatter of Lark Sings and the silvery laughter of Whippoorwill Calls.

Cat's head jerked up suddenly, and her spine stiffened. Smoke – she smelled smoke. Scrambling to her feet, she looked out across the rolling hills and saw a horseshoe of billowing smoke. A tree had been hit by lightning, and now flames leaped and danced from tree to tree.

The whole forest, full of autumn-dry timber and

papery leaves, was a tinderbox. Even as Cat watched, the horseshoe lengthened and grew, fanned by the racing wind. She saw a flaming brand sail through the air and land in a distant treetop. Within seconds, the tree was a flaming torch.

Panic gripped her chest, and smoke parched her mouth. The horseshoe of fire, as long now as a hunter's bow, was sweeping toward her with incredible speed. *I have to get out of here!* she thought with alarm. Already, she regretted coming into the forest on foot. Why hadn't she thought to bring a pony? On a pony, she would have a good chance of outrunning the fire. On foot, she would be lucky to escape the racing flames.

She scrambled out of the cave and began to run away from the fire. If only she could find a river, she thought. She had heard stories of people who waded into rivers during forest fires and survived, even when fire burned the land clear on both sides. But she knew little of this land, and she could not remember crossing a single river in the past three days.

The fire was moving away from the village. Cat breathed a sigh of relief when she realized this. But it moved toward her like a ferocious animal, devouring everything in its path and pushing her deeper and deeper into the woods.

Smoke hung thick in the air and burned the inside of her lungs. Cat could hear herself gasping with every breath. Animals took flight around her – deer and fox, rabbits and squirrels. The screaming of the birds overhead made it sound like the end of the world.

Cat ran blindly. Sweat trickled at her armpits,

and her stomach churned and heaved with fear. There was nothing about her that was human. The headstrong, self-confident tomboy named Catherine Brant was gone forever; the girl named Healing Fawn, whose heart had been touched with love, turned into smoke and vanished. She was only an animal, sobbing and leaping in a great race for survival.

The air was hot now, and the fire, like a clever enemy, stalked her at every turn. Hurtling brands had started a dozen smaller fires, and Cat began to suspect that she was hemmed in, surrounded by walls of flame. She refused to give up though even when her lungs ached and cinders burned through her moccasins.

Then, above the roar of the fire and the terrible screeching of the birds, she heard her name being called. She opened her mouth to answer, but only a strange, strangled cry came out. She licked her parched lips and tried again, running towards the voice that was calling her.

'Here I am!' she screamed. 'Here! Here!'

Blue Quail appeared in a wreath of smoke, bold and handsome as a god. His face was streaked with soot and grime, as hers was. Without a word, he rode toward her and swooped her up on to his pony.

Cat wrapped her arms around his waist and clung to him as they dodged through the smouldering trees. There was a narrow way out, but she would never forget the way the forest burned around them, the way hill after hill vanished in flames.

Blue Quail knew where a river was, and he did not stop until they reached it. Cat slid down off the pony and plunged her swollen face into the cool water. When she looked up, she saw the smoke far behind them. Blue Quail's eyes glistened like blue stones in his soot-darkened face.

'Why – how did you find me?' she asked.

'I went to see you yesterday,' he said. 'Lark Sings said you were gone, and I thought – I thought you had decided to run away. And if I never saw you again – ' He grabbed her suddenly, his hands gripping her shoulders. 'I had to find you, Fawn. I saw your tracks this morning and the fire and – '

She noticed then that two white lines – the tracks of tears – showed in his face. Standing on her tiptoes, she stopped his words with a kiss. His mouth made her lips ache, but she didn't mind. She drew back and looked up into his eyes. 'Did you really think I would try to go back – back to my people – alone?'

His eyes began to dance, and he smiled. 'A girl who would ride into battle would do almost anything, I think,' he said, proud of her courage.

But that was for you! she wanted to cry. *I only did that for you!* But she didn't have to tell him, because he was kissing her again, holding her so tightly that she believed he knew everything that was in her mind.

They would have to wait for the fire to burn itself out before they started back, Blue Quail told her. They watched all afternoon to make sure the fire was no longer chasing them. Then, near evening, they found a safe place to spend the night. Blue Quail took the blanket from his pony and folded it into a double thickness to make a soft bed for her. But Cat stubbornly unfolded the blanket, making it big enough for both of them. She saw by the look in his eyes how pleased he was.

'Are you hungry?' he asked, settling down beside her.

She snuggled against him. 'What is food?' she asked happily.

His hand stroked wisps of hair back from her forehead. 'I did not think our first home would be a rock with no roof,' he said.

Her heart soared at his words. *First home!* She trembled with delight. What a strange thing happiness was. Here she was, singed and burned and smelling like an ash heap, far from everything she had ever known, yet she was completely happy. 'I do not mind that,' she murmured, her lips grazing the warm smooth skin of his shoulder. 'I do not mind there being no roof.'

His hand caressed her cheek and neck and slid down the length of her body. He moved closer to her, and she placed her hand gently on his chest. 'There are some things, though,' she said, 'that should wait until there *is* a roof.' He rolled away from her with a sigh and lay on his back, looking up at the bright spray of stars. He said nothing, and suddenly she grew afraid – afraid that her simple refusal had somehow ended everything. She laid her head on top of his chest. 'It isn't that I don't wish to,' she said.

Then his hand was back, stroking her cheek. She turned to kiss his fingertips and laid her head in his cupped palm. When she woke in the middle of the night, his hand was tangled in her hair.

* * *

They started back the next day, riding through a charred landscape so dead and bare that it made Cat weep. Smoke still rose from the earth, and Blue Quail told her it would be days before the ground cooled. They rode for miles, the only living things in sight.

Then they reached the line of the fire, and it was like moving through a magic wall. On one side everything was dead, but on the other side the world was bursting with life. Cat pressed her cheek against Blue Quail's back. She had brought him back to the world once from death, and he had done the same for her. They had shared their lives and had been willing to share their deaths. A single bird sang above her, an invisible bird in a white birch tree. Happiness escaped her in the form of a tear, spilling out of her eye and on to his back like a raindrop.

They neared the village in the afternoon. 'Look,' Blue Quail said as they approached. He pointed to the grassy place where ponies grazed. 'Grey Lake is home. And those other ponies – he's brought Black Shoulder and One Foot Bare with him!'

Cat looked. Horses grazed among the ponies. Her back went straight as a poker. 'That's Buck!' she screamed, jumping down. 'And Dandy and Red! Those are our horses!' She looked up at him. '*Our* horses! Pa's and Ike's and James'! Don't you understand? They're here – I knew they would come. Oh!' she cried. 'They've come to take me home!'

Chapter 17

Cat sped towards the horses on foot. Seeing them was almost as good as coming within sight of her own cabin, and she rubbed her forehead against Buck's shoulder. He was the first horse she'd ever ridden, and he remembered her, turning to nuzzle her shoulder with his lips.

'Hey!' a voice behind her shouted in halting Shawnee. 'That horse is dangerous!'

Cat whirled around. 'Ike?' she said. He stared at her. She could see his mind working, trying to figure out how a Shawnee girl knew his name. 'It's me, Cat!' she shouted in English, flying towards him with open arms.

He peered at her in confusion. 'Cat? *Cat?*'

'Of course,' she said, stopping short of him, a little hurt that he hadn't recognized her. 'You *did* come here lookin' for me, didn't you?'

It began to sink in then – the person with the light braids and buckskin dress and sunburned face really was his sister. Ike Brant whooped so loudly that the ponies' ears pricked forward.

'Cat, it *is* you!' he cried, picking her up and swinging her in a wide circle. Then he set her down and surveyed her at arm's length. 'But you look a sight. I guess they made you dress that way and all. What you must have been put through. Did they torture you much?'

Cat did a double-take and saw that he was serious.

She couldn't help it – she started to laugh. 'Your mind's gone too, I reckon,' Ike added mournfully.

Cat laughed even harder. 'My mind's fine, but – oh, Ike, I have so much to tell you. Nobody tortured me at all! In fact, Blue Quail saved my life, and – ' She turned to where she'd left Blue Quail, but he was gone.

'Who's Blue Quail?' Ike asked, his eyebrows drawing together.

Cat took her brother's hand. 'Oh, Ike, I *do* have a lot to tell you,' she said, her eyes dancing. 'But where's Pa? Did James come too? How's Ma? And George and Mary? Are Joshua and Deland and William all right?'

'Stop jerking my arm thataway, Cat,' Ike said with a smile. 'You're going to jerk it right out of the socket! Everybody at home's fine, 'cept they're worried half out of their minds about you – Ma especially, of course – and Deland's got grown-up front teeth now, 'stead of gaps, and – oh, I almost forgot to tell you – you're going to be an aunt!'

Cat's eyes flew open. 'George and Mary? Already?'

Ike nodded. 'Right during planting time next spring, George figures. You'll be home by then.'

Home. For the first time, she really believed it was happening. She could almost smell the drifts of apple blossoms in the orchard. Her eyes blurred, and she blinked rapidly. 'Where's Pa?' she asked.

'Parleying with that big chief – '

'Blackfish,' Cat said.

Ike nodded. 'James is with them, too, and those other Indians – the ones we traded for and the one that came looking for 'em.'

'Grey Lake,' Cat said. 'Lark Sings will be so happy he's home. And One Foot Bare and Black Shoulder – Blackfish thought they'd be tortured to death.'

'Tortured?' Ike's eyebrows shot up. 'Those whites we got them from were kind of a sorry lot, but they certainly didn't torture them. A chief ought to know that much, at least. Oh – there was another Indian with them, too – well, sort of an Indian. A white fella in Indian clothes. He was the one that told us you were here.'

'Talks Little,' Cat said.

'I don't know,' Ike said. 'He told us his name was Richard Sloane and that he was going home.'

Cat nodded. That was Talks Little, all right.

The inside of the lodge was dim after the brilliant autumn light, but her eyes picked out the blue of the jacket gleaming with gold at the shoulders.

'Pa?' she said, her voice betraying her and fluttering like a bird's call. 'Pa? It's me.'

Ike stood behind her. 'It really *is* her, Pa. I checked, though I wouldn't have guessed it at first.'

But her father had none of Ike's doubts. 'Cat!' he cried, his deep voice rumbling like the Cumberland River in full flood. He hugged her in his big arms, the wool of his jacket scratching her cheek. 'Cat, my little girl!'

She clung to him until he put her down, but a bittersweet sadness drifted through her heart. She wasn't his little girl anymore, and never again would she be. She was grown up now, with adventures of her own and a man to love. 'I knew you'd come for me, Pa,' she said, embarrassed by the tears that spilled down her cheeks. She wiped them away with the back of her hand.

'Cat?'

She looked up. It was James, huskier than she remembered and with the first hint of a shadow on his upper lip. His voice was deepening, and, around his long-lost sister, he was suddenly shy. But she wouldn't let him be – not at such a moment. She grabbed him and hugged him. 'Oh, James. I think I missed you most of all.'

She felt her father's hand on her shoulder. 'Chief Blackfish and I were just talking about you coming home,' he said.

For the first time since she'd come into the lodge, Cat looked at the Shawnee chief. She saw now why he had always reminded her of her father. He had the same quiet self-assurance, the same ability to stand in the background without seeming insignificant. He smiled at her. 'Healing Fawn's white father has returned my sons to me – Black Shoulder and One Foot Bare. I will miss Healing Fawn much, but it is a fair trade, is it not?'

Cat saw that he was asking her to consent to the trade. Her father, Ike, and James, were looking at her as well. She bit her lip, and sweat beaded on her temples. Did she dare do what she was thinking?

It would be the biggest risk she had ever taken, one that would shape the whole course of her life. Nothing she had ever done required so much courage.

'No,' she said, forcing herself to meet each man's eyes in turn. 'It is not a fair trade. Black Shoulder and One Foot Bare are two lives. I am only one.' She swallowed. Despite the autumn chill, the air inside the lodge felt stiflingly hot against her face, as if she were again in the centre of the flaming forest. 'I will not go back unless Blue Quail goes with me.'

At first there was silence, then attempts by Cat to explain who Blue Quail was. After that, there were counter-attempts – by her father and her brothers and even Blackfish himself – to talk her out of her stubborn position. In the end, Cat insisted on talking to Blue Quail alone.

There must have been listeners outside the lodge as well, for by the time Blue Quail arrived he knew exactly what her position was. The story had circulated through the entire village.

Cat looked at him for a long moment, and he looked at her. She tried to read his thoughts but couldn't. 'Did you meet my father?' she asked. 'Did you meet Ike and James?'

'They were the ones who came to get me,' he said.

'I hope you can see what type of men they are,' she said, her eyes turning grey with determination. 'They're good men – good like Blackfish and Tecumseh. They would never ask you to be any different from what you are.' He didn't say anything, so she came around and took his hands in her own. 'Remember once how I told you that across the river from our place it's still wild? There's a hill there – a hill covered with wild plum trees, and we could build our place smack on top of it and – '

He pulled away from her. 'This,' he said, his voice shaking with emotion, '*this* is my home, Fawn. Don't you understand? This is the only world I know.'

'Except for the world we could build together,' she said stubbornly. She wouldn't let him go – she couldn't. She had risked too much, and there was no turning back. 'Do you think this world will last forever?' she asked, forcing herself to say what she believed was true, even if it hurt him. 'It won't stay as it is – even Tecumseh knows that. Wouldn't it be better to make a place all our own, a place that will last as long as we do?'

His face worked, and she glimpsed the tremendous conflict going on inside him. He said, 'But Blackfish and Tecumseh and the others – how could I leave them? Even if I wanted to, I could not walk away. They are my family.'

'They will *always* be your family,' Cat answered, 'and they will always be welcome in our home. But if you ask them, with an open heart, to tell you their thoughts, I believe they will not ask you to stay.'

Again, Blue Quail was silent. She had used her most powerful arguments. She had tried to win him away from the Shawnee with the gift of herself. But she did not know if it was enough.

'They say you have refused to return to your family unless I go also,' Blue Quail said slowly, lost in thought. 'Is that true?'

'It is true that I said it.'

'But is it true that you meant it?'

There was only one answer. 'It is true,' she told him with a sigh. 'I have no choice, Blue Quail, I love you more than my own life.'

He looked at her. She knew at once that something had changed. His eyes were clear and his face relaxed. 'Then I will go back with you, Healing

Fawn. If you love me that much, I will go back with you.' He reached out and swept her into his arms. 'On one condition,' he added.

'What?' she asked, too delighted to care what the condition was.

'That you promise never to leave me.'

She saw then that he was a little bit afraid. He had no idea of what lay ahead, and he was as frightened of her world as she had once been of his. The fact that he loved her enough to follow her anyway made her love him all the more. 'I promise,' she said, tightening her arms around him. 'I'll never leave you, not even when we're old – I won't even die before you, Blue Quail!'

'I plan to live to be very, very old,' he teased.

She set her chin in a firm line. 'The Brants live into their *hundreds*,' she replied. 'I don't plan to break the chain.' She tipped her head back and kissed him. 'I wonder what it feels like at a hundred,' she murmured.

'What what feels like?' he asked.

'Kissing. The world. Being alive.'

'It feels good enough right now,' he answered, holding her close. Cat was inclined to agree with him.

Chapter 18

Now that everything was settled, Cat was anxious to leave. Just thinking of home – of her ma bending over the fire and smoke puffing up through the chimney – made her long to be on her way. But there were preparations to make. The horses needed rest, and Blackfish insisted on sending extra food with them. They would leave in the morning, and that would be soon enough.

There was a banquet that night, and the whole village came to it. It was a bittersweet celebration, for, even though Grey Lake had brought Black Shoulder and One Foot Bare back, everyone knew that Healing Fawn and Blue Quail were leaving.

Lark Sings alternately smiled at her husband and touched his hand, ecstatic to have him safely home, and looked at Cat and cried.

'Be glad for me, Lark Sings,' Cat pleaded. 'Don't cry. Are you not happy that I'm going home?'

'Yes,' Lark Sings wept, 'but I will miss Healing Fawn.'

Then Cat herself began to cry. 'I will miss you too, Lark Sings.' She looked around the tidy lodge, where everything was in place and even the pounded dirt floor was clean. 'I will miss this place and the people in it.' That, she realized with a pang of sadness, was true.

Cat saw her father and her brothers sitting by Blackfish at the banquet. It was a place of honour, and she was glad that they seemed to realize it. Her father was talking to Blackfish in fluent Shawnee – no doubt they were swapping yarns about their great adventures. Ike looked solemn and impressed, while James, his cheeks faintly red, was busy avoiding the darting glances of Many Rainbows.

Cat took her place among the women, slipping into the space Whippoorwill Calls had saved for her. Neither of them said anything at first, but Blackfish's daughter took Cat's hand and squeezed it.

When Blue Quail appeared, Cat held her breath to see what he would do. He started towards his usual place on Blackfish's right, between Tecumseh and Loud Voice. But he caught himself, walked around to the left, and sat down beside Ike and James. Cat breathed a sigh of relief.

'They will be all right,' Whippoorwill Calls whispered beside her. *How wonderful it was to have a friend who read your thoughts.* Cat thought. And how much she would miss her! 'It will be all right,' Whippoorwill Calls repeated. 'It will all work out. You will see.'

Still, when Cat saw the first traces of awkwardness arise betwen Blue Quail and her family, she longed to rise and go to them. It was not easy to restrain herself, but she did. Blue Quail would have to make his way with her father and her brothers sometime. He might as well start now.

Blue Quail solved the problem by bringing forth a deerskin bag and offering to let them drink from it. Whippoorwill Calls nudged Cat with her elbow and raised her expressive eyebrows. *'Sofki?'* she giggled.

Cat watched the expression on her brothers' faces

as they drank – surprised at first, then delighted. '*Sofki,*' she confirmed.

By the time the deerskin bag was empty, Blue Quail seemed to have gone far towards making friends with her family.

There was dancing later, and Whippoorwill Calls was soon snatched away from Cat by Tecumseh. Cat did not stand alone for long, though, for Blue Quail came and took her hand. 'Your brothers have been telling me the most *interesting* things about you,' he said.

Cat laughed. 'There is nothing interesting about me to tell. At least, there wasn't until I met you.'

Blue Quail's eyes danced, and his smile flashed. 'Ah? Is that so? Then you were not captured running away from someone named Tom Alexander?'

'What?' Cat asked. 'They told you about him?'

A husky laugh sounded behind her. 'It's all right, Cat,' James said, flushed from the *sofki* he'd drunk. 'Tom got married about a month ago, to Becca Wells, so it's safe for you to come back.'

Cat was indignant. 'Becca Wells? Why, she isn't even pretty!'

Blue Quail looked down at her. 'You mean I'm the second warrior?' he asked. *Second warrior* meant second choice, the man a girl chose when she could not have the man she desired.

'Do not speak as if there are beetles in your head, Blue Quail,' she said, trying to hide her smile from him. 'You are my first warrior – my *only* warrior.' And she caught his hand in her own. If there had not been so many eyes watching them, she would have thrown her arms around him.

He did not let go of her hand. Drums and flute

music throbbed in their ears. 'Will Healing Fawn dance with me?' he asked.

'Yes,' Cat said, bowing her head. She was a proper Shawnee girl at last, even if it was only temporary. She shivered with happiness as Blue Quail led her into the line of dancers.

Tecumseh and Whippoorwill Calls were beside them in the line. Cat saw that they no longer made a secret of their feelings. Whippoorwill Calls' eyes were bright as black glass, and her lips, curved like a hunter's bow, were parted in an unconscious smile. Tecumseh looked at her with proud eyes. The way he looked at her and the way he took her hand as they moved through the patterns of the Shawnee dance were enough to keep other young men away.

Cat studied Blue Quail's face carefully, searching for traces of the feelings he'd once had for her beautiful friend. But those feelings, she saw, were gone. His heart was hers completely. She looked up at him with shining eyes. 'Oh,' she cried. 'I love you so much! I wish everyone would go away! I wish we could be alone together!'

He understood exactly what she meant. 'It will happen soon enough,' he told her, straining to show a patience he did not feel. His hand floated out and caressed the top of her head. 'Soon enough, Healing Fawn.'

Fog clung to the lowlands between the yellow hills. The horses, already saddled with packs and blankets, stamped and snorted with impatience. Lark Sings stood with a blanket folded around her – against the chill, she said, though Cat found the weather warm.

Until the last moment, Cat worried that Blue

Quail would change his mind, but he didn't. He mounted his pony and watched while Cat mounted hers. It was the little brown and white mare she'd ridden into battle, and Blue Quail had traded half of everything he owned to get it for her. Only the two of them knew how much the little pony meant. Years later, when the mare died of old age, they would grieve as if they'd lost one of their own children.

But that morning was far away, and this morning was close and full of the sadness of saying goodbye. Cat was surprised to see how many people came to see them off. But then, Blue Quail was a son of the village, and she was a daughter. He had raced across meadows dancing on the back of his pony, and she had healed the hand of the chief's daughter. They had done brave and exciting things, things that would be told and retold around the lodge fires for years to come. Losing them was no small matter.

Leaving Whippoorwill Calls was the hardest of all. She rubbed her cheek against Cat's and said, 'I have many brothers but only one sister. Oh, Healing Fawn, how I will miss you!'

Cat clung to her adopted sister. She too had many brothers, and no sister except for the Shawnee girl who stood before her, eyes glazed with tears. 'I will miss you, too, Whippoorwill Calls, but I will think of you every day.'

Whippoorwill Calls nodded and held up her hand. 'Look at this – the scar hardly shows.' She wiggled her fingers. 'All because of you, my sister. I will think of you always because of that.'

Cat wanted to fling herself on the ground and howl with misery. She didn't want to leave – how could she? These people had become friends and kin to her, as close as her own family. She understood then the terrible conflict that Blue Quail had felt. 'Don't cry so, Whippoorwill Calls,' she said with a fierce, thoroughly un-Shawnee hug. 'We'll see each other again.'

Whippoorwill Calls wiped her eyes. 'Of course,' she said quickly. 'I will make Tecumseh bring me to you.'

Cat nodded. They both knew it was a lie. Shawnee women seldom left their lodge fires. The idea of Whippoorwill Calls travelling hundreds of miles to visit Cat was as unlikely as the idea of Cat visiting the moon. They would never see each other again, and both of them knew it.

They set off at last, the fog lifting as the sun climbed higher. They passed the place where Blue Quail had stood pony guard and the meadow where the men and women had played ball together; they passed the golden, empty cornfields and the platform where the body of Panther Walks lay, patiently waiting for the spirits to come for him. A hard lump formed in Cat's throat.

'Healing Fawn,' a silvery voice called behind her. 'Goodbye, Healing Fawn! Goodbye!'

Cat turned and saw Whippoorwill Calls in the distance. She had raced to the top of a hill and stood there waving, tall and graceful as a plume of prairie grass. Cat waved back, tears stinging her eyes. *Oh, I will miss you! I will miss you!*

Something touched her elbow. It was Blue Quail, guiding his pony close to hers, his hand ready to lead her now to the world they would build together.

Home

It was an odd-looking place to those who didn't know it – a cabin shaped like a Shawnee lodge on top of a hill covered with wild plum trees. But no one who visited it once ever forgot it. Happiness spilled out of its crooked little windows and puffed up through the roof with the chimney smoke.

It was the place that Blue Quail and his wife built together in the spring of 1788. The idea of using logs and mud daubing in the walls had been Cat's. 'Shawnee lodges are good,' she admitted with a firm set to her jaw, 'but they get rebuilt every year. I want a house that will last as long as we do.'

Blue Quail, noting the line of her jaw and the steel blue of her eyes, decided to agree with her. But he kept to his own plans for the shape of the place – he wanted a domed roof that would shed snow in the winter and sun in the summer.

The Brants ferried across the Cumberland River with Cat and Blue Quail to help with the building, and none of them much minded how the house was shaped. Cat, their tomboy, had gone off and found herself someone as full of flint as she was. Watching them quarrel and make up over how the house was to be built filled them all with laughter.

Everything and everyone cooperated with building the cabin – even the weather, which was fair and dry. Cat stood on her front porch – a huge flat stone she'd found in the forest – and sniffed the breeze, scented with plum blossoms. *This is home*, she said to herself.

The only person who didn't cooperate with the building was little John Brant, George and Mary's firstborn, who arrived in the middle of everything, making Cat an aunt. But the cabin was finished anyway – a fine, sturdy place. In ten years' time, when their family had grown, a larger house was built, a proper two-storey cabin with a gabled roof. The little round-topped lodge became a barn, then a storehouse, and finally a house again for the youngsters who thought themselves old enough to sleep away from the big cabin.

The wedding came after the cabin was finished, on a day so warm and beautiful that Cat longed to take off her stiff new shoes and run around barefoot. (She did do this, in fact, but not until the minister had spoken and she was properly married.)

The only trouble was with the names. Was she to be Mrs Blue Quail. Mrs Quail, or something else? Her husband solved everything by volunteering to take his wife's name. He didn't remember his own white name, he said, and if Brant was good enough for Cat, it would be good enough for him too. Even so, they were always strange about names, calling each other Shawnee names long after Blue Quail had mastered the English language. Later, when they had children, they picked strange names for them too: their oldest boy was named Quail, and their daughter was Whippoorwill.

Cat and her husband were a wild pair in their young days. They fled their new lodge on their wedding night and rode deep into the woods for their honeymoon, finding secret new places and sleeping under the moonlight. When their friends and relatives showed up to shivaree them, they found an empty cabin.

Cat and Blue Quail laughed a lot about this – about the friends and neighbours who went banging on the walls and windows of a empty house. It was exactly like them not to be home, not to be where they were expected, to be off in a world of their own.

AFTERWORD
An Historical Note

Cat and Blue Quail are fictional, but they might well have existed in the America of the late 1780s. Their home wasn't called Kentucky then, but *Kaintuck* – the Indian name for it. It was a wild and beautiful country, and for a long time it had been the hunting ground of the Indians.

It is easy to see, then, why the Shawnee saw the white settlers who pushed into the region as trespassers. Spilling down from the north and across from the east in the years that followed the American Revolution, few of them stopped to ask whom the land belonged to or what the consequences of settling it might be. People like Cat and Blue Quail were drawn into the bitter struggle, separated from their families for years or – in some cases – for their entire lives.

Tecumseh, who was a real person, went on to become chief. In spite of his fame, very little is known about him, including the meaning of his name. We do know that at a very early age he lost his real father, who was killed in battle, and he and his brothers were adopted and raised by the great chief Blackfish. When Tecumseh was a teenager, his favourite older brother was also killed in battle.

These sad losses shaped Tecumseh's thinking as he was growing up. He quickly proved himself to be a fine warrior and a respected leader. Early in his adulthood, he began to argue for a strong and independent Shawnee nation.

Tecumseh's brother Loud Voice was also real. He shared Tecumseh's vision of Indian unity and became known as the Prophet – the spiritual leader of the Shawnee.

Although Tecumseh himself was killed in battle in 1813, he left his mark upon his people, who made a valiant attempt to fulfill his vision. Today, there are Shawnee descendants who meet every year to celebrate the old traditions and pass them along to their children.

I have tried to weave into this book what little we know of the Shawnee and their culture. They were a magnificent people, with a complex and well-organized society. Everyone's work was valuable and required, and everyone participated when it was time for fun. The ball game, in which Cat and Whippoorwill Calls played against Blue Quail and the men, was an established fact of life. The corn dance also existed, as did the sweet, intoxicating drink called *sofki*.

Prisoners of the Shawnee fared far better than prisoners of many other tribes. For the most part, the Shawnee treated captives with respect and even kindness. If a family adopted a white person, as Blackfish adopted Cat, Blue Quail, and Talks Little, it was without prejudice. The adopted person was given the same rights as anyone else. Many captives, taken in infancy or youth, lived their whole lives as Shawnee. If Blue Quail had not decided to return to Kentucky with Cat, he might eventually have risen to the level of a chief.

It saddens me that so much of the Shawnee culture

has been lost. When the white settlers came, they were so busy with their own struggles that they didn't see or think to save what had gone before them. This book has been my way of trying to see what my ancestors did not see.

Meg Cameron